Saving His Soul

Dawn Sullivan

Published by Dawn Sullivan

Cover Design: Kari Ayasha-Cover to Cover Designs

Photographer: Shauna Kruse-Kruse Images & Photography

Models: William Scott and T. H. Snyder

Language: English

Dedication

I have always been a dreamer. Even as a child, I would make up stories about far-off fantasy places. I would pretend I was the heroine, meeting my handsome prince and falling in love. You hardly ever saw me without a book in my hand. Now, I write because I love to. I enjoy getting swept up in a story, dreaming about my characters and their lives. And, yes, once again, I'm that heroine for as long as the book lasts.

This one is for all of the dreamers out there; the ones who have their head in the clouds and one foot on the ground. Always follow your dreams. Fight for them, and live life to the fullest.

Other books by Dawn Sullivan

RARE Series

Book 1 Nico's Heart
Book 2 Phoenix's Fate
Book 3 Trace's Temptation
Book 4 Saving Storm

White River Wolves Series

Book 1 Josie's Miracle
Book 2 Slade's Desire

Serenity Springs Series

Book 1 Tempting His Heart
Book 2 Healing Her Spirit

Chapter 1

Six years ago

Sitting in a darkened corner of the small bar, she watched him as he lightly strummed the guitar strings. His black cowboy hat covered dark blond hair and was pulled down low on his forehead. His head was bowed, hiding his face. All she could see was his strong, chiseled jaw, but she knew what the rest of his features looked like. She had them memorized. Even after six long years, she would know him anywhere.

When the deep timbre of Ryder Caldwell's voice filled the room, she leaned forward in her chair, listening intently. The song was a slow ballad about love lost, and she clung to every word, pretending he was singing to her.

Suddenly, Ryder raised his head and glanced around the room. She gasped when his gaze stopped on her, before slowly moving on. Those eyes. She had always loved his mesmerizing, bright blue eyes. They had the power to make her heart race and her palms sweat. She froze when his gaze came back and settled on her again.

Shit, she could not let him see her. She was not even supposed to be there. The chance of him recognizing her after so many years was slim, but it was one she was not willing to take. There was no way she would bring the terror that she lived with daily into his life. When he once again lowered his gaze to his guitar, she took a chance and slid from the booth, quickly leaving the bar without a backward glance.

Chapter 2

Present Time

Rayna Williams knelt by the gravesite, gently placing a single long-stemmed red rose on the ground before her. Gazing at the small headstone above where the rose lay, she reached out and lightly traced the name, Matthew James Fuller. Tears filled her eyes as she remembered the young boy, full of love and laughter. Matty was taken way too soon from this world, never having the chance to learn to drive, to go on his first date, to fall in love, get married, or have children of his own.

Moving to the next gravesite, she repeated the action of tracing the name on the headstone, a shudder racking her body as she held back a scream of agony that wanted to tear from her throat. Leaving the rose, she moved on to the next grave, and then the next. They were all gone, had been for years, but the pain of losing them was just as deep and sharp as it had been right after they were taken from her.

Placing the last rose on the ground, Rayna rose, standing stiffly in front of the large headstone before her parents' graves. It was now just over twelve years since the terrible accident that had stolen her entire family from her, but it still felt like only yesterday. When she lost them, it was as if she lost a piece of herself. A part she was afraid she would never get back.

Closing pain-filled eyes, Rayna felt a tear escape as she whispered softly, "I miss all of you so much." The life that she lived since the accident was a lonely one. She was too afraid to let anyone get close to her. She refused to be the cause of more death.

Taking a deep breath, Rayna opened her eyes, wiping tears from them as she let her gaze rest on the family headstone. She read the engraving once again, even though she knew it by heart.

Here lies the Fuller family

Father: Robert Fuller

Mother: Rosemary Fuller

Daughter: Olivia Fuller

Daughter: Macey Fuller

Son: Matthew Fuller

May they rest in peace

Out of all of them, she was the only one left. Her breath hitching on a silent sob, Rayna squeezed her eyes shut tightly as the memory of that terror-filled night swamped her. She recalled the phone ringing, the panic in her father's voice when he ordered them all to the car, not allowing them to pack a suitcase or even retrieve any of their personal possessions first. She and her sister were both old enough to understand what was going on, having gone through it once before, but Matthew was only a baby when they were moved the first time. He had been so scared. She remembered holding his hand tightly while her sister cried softly in the seat next to him.

Her mother turned to look at them from where she sat in the passenger seat, tears flowing freely down her cheeks, her dark green eyes wide with fear. "It's going to be alright," she promised as she clutched the back of the seat. "Everything is going to be just fine." She had talked quietly to them for several miles, but in the end, all of her promises did not matter.

Rayna remembered the screeching of metal, bright lights, and then gut-wrenching screams from her mother. Her dad was yelling, telling them all to duck down. Suddenly, the back window shattered, and she saw her father slump forward onto the steering wheel. The car careened out of control, slamming into something before turning onto its side and skidding across the highway. After it finally came to a stop, there was complete silence. Everything went absolutely still, and it was as if time slowed down. Matty lay lifelessly on her, her sister on top of him. She struggled to move, but could not under their combined weight. Her head was pounding, blood dripping down her forehead and into her eyes. She moaned softly as dizziness overcame her, trying to remain conscious.

That was when she heard footsteps coming toward the car. Frozen in fear, Rayna fought to keep quiet, her body trembling in terror as she squeezed her eyes tightly shut. She struggled not to scream when the sound of five more gunshots cracked through the night. A sharp pain pierced her shoulder and she let out a muffled cry, then once again silence filled the air. After a moment she heard a voice say gruffly, "It's done, boss," right before she slipped into oblivion.

Several hours later, Rayna woke up in a hospital over a thousand miles from Serenity Springs, Texas, where she was told that she was the only survivor of the crash and what transpired after it. Her entire family was now resting in the burial plots before her. The U.S. Marshals in charge of her safety would not even consider letting her attend the funeral. They set it up to look as if all five family members perished in the accident, burying an empty casket before her headstone.

Two days following the accident, she was once again relocated with another new name, Rayna

Williams. It was her third name, counting the one she was born with, and she vowed it would be the final one. Five days following her relocation, she found out that the mob boss who ordered the hit on her family had his henchmen dig up all of the graves. He wanted proof that the job was done. What they found when they got to hers, was an empty casket. Rayna knew the bastard would not rest until she was gone, because he left her a message in that casket after discovering she was still alive. It was the dead body of her last living relative, Aunt Silvia.

Rayna had lived with the horror of that night for the past twelve years. Everything she did from that point on was so that she could make it through day-by-day, knowing the bastards were still out there and gunning for her. She made the decision to go into law enforcement, determined to be able to protect herself and those she cared about, not that there was anyone in her life to look out for right now. There had been some who tried to get close to her, but she always ended up pushing them all away. Yes, she lived a lonely existence, but at least she knew no one else would suffer if she was found by her enemies.

Originally, Rayna wanted to become a U.S. Marshal so that she could protect others who had been through hell and back, like herself. In the end, she decided against it, changing her career path to focus on hunting down the bastards who threatened them instead. After two years as a police officer, followed by three as a detective on the police force in Omaha, Nebraska where she was living at the time, she now worked for the Federal Bureau of Investigations in Virginia. Her past files were sealed, buried so deep that no one besides the U.S. Marshals knew her life story, except the director and assistant director of the FBI. And the only reason they knew was because Rayna chose to tell the assistant director before he hired her. In her mind, honesty was the best policy, and she wanted him to be able to make his decision with all of the facts. That was two years ago. Since then, she had worked her ass off for the bureau, and was now a valued agent.

Even though things in her life seemed to be going well right now, Rayna recently made a decision, one that was a long time coming. She was done running. She refused to hide. She was going back to the only place that ever felt like home. It was time to face her demons, time to fight.

Taking a deep breath, Rayna squared her shoulders and said out loud, "I know you probably won't understand, Mama. You always said I was the headstrong one of the bunch. But this is something that I have to do. I'm tired of looking over my shoulder. Tired of wondering if those bastards are still hunting me. If they are, they can come find me, and I plan on making it easy for them. I'm going back to Serenity Springs, Mama. I'm going home."

After one last glance at the dark red roses she had left on four out of five of the gravesites, Rayna turned and made her way to the black, four-door Charger parked on the side of the road. She had purposely neglected to place a rose on her own grave. It was an open invitation. *Come find me, you bastards.*

Chapter 3

"Your leave of absence has been denied," Assistant Director Talbot informed Rayna as he stared across his desk at her, a knowing look in his shrewd grey eyes.

"With all due respect, Sir," Rayna demanded, "by whom?" Her anger was at a slow burn and was quickly catching fire. She had waited years to be free of that scum, Diego Cortez, and she was not going to let anything stand in her way now that she was finally ready to confront him. Forcing herself to remain seated, she gritted her teeth and waited for Talbot to respond.

"By me, Agent Williams," the assistant director stated as he rose from his chair and walked around his desk, stopping before her. "Rayna," he said calmly, "I know what you have planned, and I can't allow it."

Rayna's dark brown eyes narrowed as she replied shortly, "I'm tired. I need a vacation."

"Bullshit," Talbot scoffed as he leaned back against his desk, folding his arms across his wide chest. "You forget, Rayna Williams, that I know you better than anyone else." When she refused to comment, he continued, "You have been keeping close tabs on Diego Cortez for the past year, making sure you have all of his current information at your fingertips. You've been stalking the small town of Serenity Springs via the internet for close to six months now, if not longer. Last month, the house you grew up in went up for sale. According to county records, it is now owned by a Rayna Williams. The utilities are also in your name. And now you want to take an indefinite leave of absence? How stupid do you think I am, Rayna?"

"You've been watching me." It was a statement, not a question. Rayna really didn't give a damn, though. She had not even bothered to cover her tracks. If she wanted to, it would have been child's play. She had always been good with computers, which was how she figured out that there was a leak in the FBI. Every few days, she would log on and check to see if there was anyone out there trying to hack into her sealed files. The answer was always no, until just a few months ago. That was when she knew she was no longer safe, although safe was not a word Rayna had known in over twenty years.

Instead of waiting for whoever was stalking her to figure out exactly who she was, Rayna decided to become the hunter instead of the hunted. She came up with a plan and began to leave a trail carefully, beginning with when she became Rayna Williams, to her work with the FBI, and then finally to her decision to move home to Serenity Springs. This was where she planned on ending her life long battle with Cortez, one way or another.

"I watch all of my agents," Assistant Director Talbot growled, his eyes darkening with his own anger. "What makes you think I am going to allow you to cut ties with the bureau, and run off to face the likes of Cortez on your own like some kind of modern day vigilante?"

"I'm not cutting ties with anyone," Rayna denied, and she wasn't. She liked her job, liked the life she had made for herself. There was only one thing missing, but he'd been lost to her years ago, even before the accident. Once she took care of Cortez, Rayna was selling her family home and finally placing that part of her life behind her. If she lived, that was. "I'll be back in a few months. I just need a little time off."

"Well, you aren't going to get it," Talbot informed her as he stood and walked back around the desk to once again take a seat in his large, black leather chair.

"Dammit, Ethan!" Rayna snapped as she rose, placing her hands on her hips. "That son of a bitch killed my family. He has been after me for years, and won't stop until I'm dead. I am done waiting for him to find me."

"I didn't say you were going to wait, Agent Williams. I said I wasn't sending you off on your own."

Rayna froze, lowering back down into her seat as his meaning sank in. The assistant director was not going to keep her from ending this thing with Diego Cortez, he was going to help her. Swallowing hard, she said, "I appreciate that, Sir, but I don't want to place anyone else's lives in danger. Cortez wants me, and he doesn't care who he has to go through to get to me." When he would have responded, Rayna held up a hand. "I also don't know who I can trust here. Someone has been trying to access my old case files from the database."

Leaning forward, the director rested his forearms on the large desk. "Your records here should have been buried way too deep for someone to find." His brow furrowing, he growled, "I'll see if Agent Hanson can figure out who was trying to get into your files. In the meantime, I want you to bring Agents Donaldson and Brentworth up to speed on the situation." Before Rayna could protest, the director shook his head. "No excuses, Rayna. It's time you start trusting people." Rayna looked down to where her hands sat tightly clasped in her lap, but her gaze snapped back to the director's when he continued, "Just as we are going to trust you."

"What do you mean?"

"The FBI has been keeping tabs on Cortez for years. I was already working for the agency when your father came to us. I was just a rookie at the time, still wet behind the ears. I thought I was going to save the world." Shaking his head at the idea, he went on, "I was at my desk when Mr. Fuller walked in, scared to death for his family, but prepared to do what was right. Before you ask, I was not the agent assigned to your father's case. My team was handling another large case at the time. But bringing down Cortez was a huge thing. And we were so damn close."

"Until he somehow got off on a technicality after Dad testified," Rayna said woodenly. She was so young at the time, but she still remembered the agony and terror in her father's voice when he found out Diego Cortez had walked. Then the death threats started, but nothing could be traced back to Cortez. After an attempt was made on their lives, the U.S. Marshals stepped in and removed the Fullers from the area, leaving behind no traces of them…or so they thought.

"It turned out the judge was in his pocket," the assistant director admitted. "Not only that, but the jury was scared shitless to go up against the mob boss."

"Why do you think the verdict will be any different now?" Rayna questioned, even though she knew if it came down to putting a bullet in the bastard or bringing him in to stand trial, she would do the latter. "What makes you think we can finally put him away?"

"A couple of things. We have some movers and shakers in Washington now. They want this case closed as much as I do. They will do anything to get Diego behind bars." A slow smile curved Talbot's lips as he continued, "Diego has lost a lot of his following in the D.C. area, which you know. His organization should have grown over time, but instead has actually dwindled significantly in numbers. Everyone is terrified of him. They don't want to work for him because they are afraid they will be the next dead body to show up in the river." His eyes glittering with determination, he said, "As much as I hate the idea of using you as bait, you are the only person in his past that could lure him out of hiding who isn't already six feet under. I don't think that we will be able to make a move on him here on his home turf, but the Director and I both agree that with our agents integrated in Serenity Springs to back you up, we have a good chance of catching the bastard."

"With all due respect, Sir, Diego may be a crazy son of a bitch, and he may have lost some of his empire, but that doesn't make him stupid. You know as well as I do that he is still watching Serenity Springs to see if I will return. You can't just suddenly stick a number of agents into a town that size and think he's not going to notice. Especially if I show up around the same time."

Talbot stared at her intently as he idly tapped his fingers on the desk in front of him. "I agree. That's why we are only sending two other agents and we are going to work with the Serenity Springs Police Department on this one."

"No!" Rayna's response was quick and forceful. "You will not involve the Caldwells in this. I won't allow it."

The Assistant Director raised an eyebrow, a smirk on his hard lips. "*You* won't allow it, Agent Williams? Let me remind you who is in charge here. I might be agreeing to this foolhardy plan, and against my better judgment, I am allowing you to be a part of it. But, make no mistake, I am the one in charge. I will involve whoever I think needs to be involved."

Rayna sat quietly, her dark eyes snapping in anger. She wanted to get Diego, had wanted to catch the bastard for years, but not at the expense of innocent lives. Finally, when she was sure her emotions were once again under control, she implored, "Please, Ethan, don't involve the Caldwells. They are a good family. An innocent family. They don't deserve to be brought back into my nightmare."

"Back into it?" Talbot asked. "What the hell is that supposed to mean?"

Rayna refused to tell her superior everything about her past. She would keep him informed on what he needed to know, but some things were just too personal to share. "I know them from my time at Serenity Springs. I don't want any of them hurt. Please, I'm asking you, don't involve them in this."

Sighing deeply, Talbot replied, “I’m sorry, Rayna, but it’s too late. Once I figured out what your intentions were, I contacted the Sheriff in Serenity Springs. I informed him of the situation and our plans. He’s on board with everything.”

“That’s it? It was that easy? You tell Creed Caldwell that we are going to draw the fucking mob to his home town, and he was fine with it? I find that hard to believe.”

Laughing sardonically, Talbot shook his head. “Of course not. He was pissed as hell. But, when he found out I was going to do it anyway and there was nothing he could do about it, he demanded that he be fully involved with the investigation.”

“Does he know who I am?” Rayna asked softly.

“No. He only knows what he needs to know.”

“I think he needs to know everything,” Rayna whispered, against her better judgment. “As much as I want to keep the whole operation as far away from Creed Caldwell and his family as possible, if you are going to insist on the police department’s involvement, then he needs to know.” God, she did not want to do this. She did not want to bring the pain and horror of her life into the lives of the Caldwells. She had no idea how this suicide mission of hers would turn out. In a perfect world, she would bring Diego Cortez to justice, but she had been shown several times in the past that the world she lived in was far from perfect.

"Then I will leave it up to you to tell them," the Assistant Director decided, once again rising from his seat. "Now, go meet with Donaldson and Brentworth. They can bring you up to speed on everything we have on Cortez. If you know anything we do not, share it with them. Then, the three of you need to devise a plan. Work together on this, Rayna. It is the only way we are going to get the bastard."

Rayna stood and walked slowly toward the door, her mind focused on the task before her. She had come into the meeting expecting her request for a leave of absence to be approved. She was packed and ready to go, and planned on leaving tomorrow morning with no idea whether she would really return or not. Now, all of her plans would need to be changed. Not only was the FBI involved in her fight, but so was the Serenity Springs Police Department. She knew three of the Caldwell siblings worked for that police department. She refused to think about one specific Caldwell who had captured her heart so long ago; the way his intense blue gaze would brighten with laughter and his lips would turn up in a slow, sexy grin as he teased her mercilessly. Her young heart had warmed towards him and she had begun to live for the time that she was able to spend in his presence. Her hands tightening into fists, she vowed that she would protect the Caldwell family from the evil that stalked her. She would protect them all, no matter what.

"Rayna." Turning back to acknowledge the Assistant Director, she waited patiently for him to continue. "This will not be easy. Diego Cortez will not go down without a fight. But, I want you to know, this agency will stand behind you the whole way. You are a good person, Rayna Williams, and an outstanding agent. I have no doubt that we *are* going to bring Cortez down this time."

That makes one of us, Rayna thought sarcastically. That bastard always managed to stay just below the radar somehow. There was so much death and destruction on his hands, but her father had been the only person with enough courage to stand up to him. That courage had gotten Rayna's entire family killed. Well, payback was a bitch. And Rayna was all about payback when it came to that piece of shit.

"Stay safe, Rayna," Talbot said gruffly.

"I will," she replied shortly before turning to go meet with Donaldson and Brentworth. They were seasoned agents with a lot of experience under their belts. If anyone could help her capture Cortez, it would be them.

Ethan Talbot sat back down in his chair, heaving a huge sigh of frustration. Rearranging a stack of papers on his desk, he swore quietly. He hated sending an agent to what could very possibly be her death. He wasn't lying when he told Rayna she was an outstanding agent. She had proven herself more than once with the bureau, and was one of the best agents he'd ever worked with. Not only that, but she was strong, loyal, and full of determination. He did not want to lose her.

Squeezing the bridge of his nose tightly, he groaned softly before reaching for the phone. A moment later he was being transferred to the Director of the FBI. "Talk to me," Director Anderson demanded as soon as he answered the call.

His grip tightening on the phone, Ethan told him, "It was exactly what we thought. She was going to lure the bastard to her. Who knows what she had planned for Cortez once she got ahold of him."

"We both know what she planned," the director scoffed, "and if I wasn't worried that she would get herself killed in the process, I would let her do it."

"She might still end up dead," Ethan said gruffly, as he fidgeted with his pen. He really did not want Rayna's death on his conscience.

"You have a couple of your best agents going in with her you said. She has a much better chance now than she did just hours ago."

Throwing the pen across the room, Ethan snarled, "I know, but this is still a fucking suicide mission. You and I both know it. My agents can't be with her 24/7. And if I send more than the two that I chose, chances are Cortez will make them right away if he has eyes on the town. I have to keep the number down because Serenity Springs is so small. I don't have a choice."

"What are the undercover assignments of the agents you are sending?" the Director asked.

Ethan stiffened, sitting up straight in his chair. Up to this point, he had refused to tell anyone except Donaldson and Brentworth which agents were going and exactly what they would be doing. He knew even before Rayna told him that there was a leak in the agency. And, even though he was sure the Director was clean, he was still going to keep the information quiet. "I have to go, Ben," he said quickly when his cell phone rang. "I have another call."

Ignoring the Director's sputtered response, Ethan hung up the phone and then silenced the ringing on his cell. Picking his office phone back up, he dialed Agent Hanson's extension. The man was a genius with computers. If anyone could track who was trying to get information on Rayna, he could.

Chapter 4

Rayna stood outside the door of the conference room where Senior Field Agents Donaldson and Brentworth waited for her. She was hesitant to enter after her conversation with Talbot. Before, in her plan to take down Diego, she was the only one involved, which meant the only one she had to worry about keeping alive was herself. Now, after her conversation with the assistant director, there were not only two more FBI agents involved, but also the Caldwell family. And even though it may be the FBI's job to take down criminals like Diego, the Caldwells had not signed up for this. Defending the small town of Serenity Springs was a lot different than going up against the biggest mob in the Washington D.C. area. Unfortunately, it was too late. There was no way Talbot would let her go off on her own now that he knew what she was up to.

She knew she should be grateful that the Bureau was backing her crazy scheme, but somehow everything changed when the Caldwells became a part of the picture. Rayna still wanted to confront the man who had ruined her life, and she was positive the only way to draw him out into the open so that she could get to him, was to lure him to Serenity Springs. But, her fear for the family she had once cared for was making her hesitate. If something happened to one of them, she would never forgive herself.

Rayna reached out and grasped the doorknob firmly. Taking a deep breath, she turned it and swung the door open. The other agents looked up from the files spread out on the table in front of them as she entered the room. She found herself trembling under the hard gaze of Agent Nathan Brentworth as she closed the door behind her. He sat at the end of the table, a man who seemed to immediately demand the attention of anyone who walked into the room. He was a legend in her field, after taking down more criminals than she could ever imagine doing herself. His specialty was working undercover in many different capacities because of his ability to blend in wherever he was needed. She knew he was in his late forties, but he was able to assume an identity from age twenty-five to over fifty. She also knew that once the man went undercover, you would not recognize him unless he wanted you to. Right now he had a distinguished look about him, with his dark black hair slightly greying in spots, cleanly shaven face, and dark suit and tie that looked custom-made just for him. Vaguely, she wondered how many kill shots he had under his belt. Personally, even though there were many dicey situations where she came close, she'd never actually had to put a bullet in another person. However, she was certain that was about to change.

Letting her gaze wander from the steel grey eyes of the man in front of her, she glanced over to where Agent Donaldson sat in a chair at the middle of the table, across from where Rayna stood. The woman smiled gently, before motioning to the seat in front of her. "Please, have a seat." Her light blue gaze was filled with a warmth that surprised Rayna, because she knew the other agent had worked for the FBI for over thirty years. She thought a seasoned agent such as Kayla Donaldson would be…harder. Kayla tended to spend more time in the office now than in the field, running down leads and going over theories with a team that worked under her, but Rayna was not fooled. She'd seen Agent Donaldson in action at one point, and never wanted to be on her bad side.

Rayna sat where the other woman indicated, leaning forward and resting her arms on the table. Glancing back and forth at the agents, she introduced herself, "I'm Agent Rayna Williams. It's nice to meet you."

"We know who you are," Brentworth said, with a short nod.

Agent Donaldson smiled, "We've seen your file, Rayna. It's very impressive. We are happy to have you on our team."

"Thank you, Agent Donaldson," Rayna replied, not sure if she should be pissed that they took the liberty to look at her file, or happy they found her acceptable to work with.

“Please, call me Kayla.”

“How much do you know about Diego Cortez?” Agent Brentwood interrupted in a deep, gravelly voice. Before she could reply, he picked up a file in front of him and tossed it towards her. “The guy is scum. He takes lives like they mean nothing to him. We have been trying to bring him down for years, and now Talbot says we have a good chance of getting the job done.”

“I know everything there is to know about Diego Cortez,” Rayna responded roughly. “I have made it a priority to find out every single thing about him that I could over the past few years.”

Her eyes narrowing, Kayla asked, “And why is that?”

“The assistant director didn’t tell you?” Even though it frustrated Rayna, she was not surprised. It would seem as if he were going to leave it up to her to share her story. Maybe it was his way of protecting her, she didn’t know. What she did know was that if these two people were going to help her, then they needed to know the truth.

Opening the file in front of her, she flipped through it until she found what she was looking for. Turning it around, she pointed at it. “You tell me. How much do you know about the Fuller case?”

Kayla stiffened as she reached out and lightly touched the file, tracing a finger over the picture of the Fuller family clipped inside. "Everything," she finally whispered, raising pain-filled eyes back up to meet Rayna's gaze. "I was a part of the investigation. The father came to us, ready to testify and put Diego Cortez away. Things didn't work out the way we all hoped. After Cortez went free, we put the family in protective custody with new names, in a place we thought he would never find them. We were wrong. Not only did he track them down, but he killed them. All of them. He murdered them because the father was brave enough to stand up against the bastard in court."

"Not all of them," Rayna said softly.

"What?" Agent Brentworth growled. "That's not true. I was there, dammit. I went to their funeral. It was one of the only cases in my career where I fucking failed. I failed that family. I let that son of a bitch kill them. I failed every single one of them."

"No you didn't," Rayna told him, her eyes meeting his stormy grey ones.

"Yes I did, dammit," he snapped, slamming his fist into the table. "They had kids. Two teenage girls and a little boy, and I didn't protect them."

"How could you have?" Rayna asked incredulously. "The FBI was not even involved with them after the trial."

"No, but I should have done something in the beginning," he insisted, "before the trial was thrown out."

"What?" Rayna demanded. "What could you have done? There was nothing you could have done, Nathan, nothing."

His eyes widened in surprise at the use of his first name, but she didn't care. She had never seen him look the way that he did right now. So upset, torn up, beaten. She could not just sit there and let the man torment himself.

"I went to their funeral," he snarled. "Five caskets, all closed because the destruction was too much for people to see. Five caskets containing bodies of people that I could not protect."

"You see," Rayna said softly, "that is where you are wrong." Looking at both of them, she smiled tremulously. "There were only four bodies in those caskets."

"What?" Kayla sat up straighter in her chair, leaning forward earnestly. "What are you saying?"

"There were only four bodies," Rayna repeated, her gaze going back and forth between the two agents. "I survived."

There was complete silence in the room. After a long moment, Nathan finally spoke. "You were one of the girls?"

"Yes," Rayna admitted. "I was taken by the U.S. Marshals from the accident, and my name was changed again. They put me back in witness protection with a whole new identity."

"But, I don't understand," Kayla said in confusion. "How are you an FBI agent? How are you even in law enforcement at all? I wouldn't think the U.S. Marshals would allow it. The people they put in witness protection are supposed to get jobs where no one would think to look for them. Teachers, construction workers, convenience store clerks, things like that. They are not supposed to be waving around guns and calling attention to themselves."

Rayna let out a short laugh as she crossed her arms over her chest. "Yeah, they tried that with me," she said with a shrug. "I never have listened very well. I've always been one to travel my own path. Quiet, but determined." She smiled as she remembered how it always drove her mother crazy. She used to say that Rayna was too stubborn for her own good. Smiling wryly at the memory, Rayna went on, "They had me hidden in a small town in Nebraska, close to Omaha. I finished college and applied to the police force. I was accepted before the Marshals knew what was going on. I didn't ask anyone's permission, I just did it."

"It didn't raise any red flags when they did a background check on you?"

Rayna shook her head. "After what happened to my family, everything in my past was completely erased and my files buried deeply, so deeply only the

U.S. Marshals would know the truth. They gave me a whole new background, all the way back to my birth. Some of those computer programmers on staff are geniuses. They can work miracles."

"What about when you took the lie detector test?"

"They didn't ask me anything that I actually had to lie about. There is a way around everything." It had been much more difficult to get past that test than she was letting on, but she'd managed it. "The U.S. Marshals tried to get me to quit when they found out what I was doing, but I refused." Looking down at the table, Rayna slowly tapped her fingertips against the dark wood. "You know, when I was younger, I had my life all planned out. I knew exactly what I wanted to be when I grew up. I even knew who I wanted to marry, and how many kids we would have. My life has turned out nothing like I planned. The accident that night, what Diego Cortez did to me and my family, changed everything. I worked hard to become the person I am today, so that I could bring that bastard down not only for what he did to my family, but for what he has done to so many other innocent people. And now, I am getting my chance."

"Why Serenity Springs?" Nathan wanted to know.

"He's been looking for me," Rayna admitted. "There's a leak here in the office." She held a hand up to stop the questions she knew were coming. "I don't know who it is, but I do know there is one. I'm going to draw Diego back to Serenity Springs, without letting him know that I am. I have started to leave subtle hints about who I used to be, and who I have become. I want him to find me. Originally, my plan was to take a leave of absence from work. I bought the house my family lived in before the accident, and I was going to lure him back to Serenity Springs. I knew it could take months for him to show up, but I was willing to wait."

"What made you think the FBI would take you back if you went rogue like that?" Kayla asked incredulously.

Rayna returned the other woman's gaze steadily, but did not reply.

"She didn't think she would be coming back," Nathan said quietly. "She planned on following through with her plan, whether she ended up dead or alive."

Rayna nodded, "I figured I would jump that hurdle if I got to it. I had no idea how long my mission would take."

Running a hand through his thick, dark hair, Nathan said, "Talbot told us that you were going in to draw Cortez out. He never gave us the full story behind it, and we were trying to figure out why he thought you would be able to attract the mob's attention. Now we know."

"The assistant director said he was sending two agents in undercover with me. Is that you?"

"Not me," Kayla replied. "I don't do that kind of work anymore. I tend to stay in the office, with the occasional offsite field work. Nathan will be going, along with Lyssa Taylor."

Lyssa Taylor, Rayna thought. She was a newer agent, but a very good one who held a lot of promise.

"Where will the two of you be?" she asked Nathan.

"I'll be working at a place called New Hope Ranch. It's a few miles outside of town and close to your old farm."

"I know it," Rayna responded, surprised he would choose New Hope to stay at. "It's a home for troubled kids run by Harper Daley. She started it after her husband passed away a few years ago. Harper's going to let you work there? I would think she would be worried about putting the children in danger."

"They won't be in any kind of danger," Nathan promised, sliding his chair back from the table and standing to stretch. "And Harper has no idea why I will be there. She thinks I am just a rancher looking for a job. Our people gave me a good resume. It's iron clad. She has no reason to suspect I'm there for anything except to work with the horses, and sometimes the children."

Rayna sighed, "You better hope so, Brentworth, because I can tell you right now, if anything happens to one of those kids, Harper will string you up by your balls."

Before he could respond, Kayla interjected, "Lyssa will be working at Mac's Diner as a waitress. She starts tomorrow, and is staying in an apartment above the diner. Both she and Nathan will blend in nicely, and I will be here with eyes on Cortez."

Nathan stalked to the door, opening it before looking back, "Be here tomorrow morning at 7 a.m. sharp. We have some major planning to do before we send you in."

Rayna sighed deeply, as she watched him go. He was right. If they were going to pull this off, and she would or die trying, then they needed to go over every detail, piece by piece. Even if that meant that she would arrive in Serenity Springs a few days behind schedule.

Chapter 5

Ryder removed his Stetson and wiped the sweat from his brow with the shirt he'd stripped off over an hour ago. The sun was out in full force and it was only midmorning. He had been fixing fence since 4 a.m. to try and beat the heat, but it wasn't working.

Walking back over to where his gelding stood waiting patiently, Ryder removed a bottle of water from the saddlebag and took a long drink. Tilting his head back, he dumped the rest of the water over his face and down his body to try and cool off. After replacing his Stetson, he put the empty bottle back in the bag and went back to the fence to gather up his tools. He was supposed to report for duty at the station in an hour, and he desperately needed a shower first. Ryder knew he was cutting it close, but some of the cattle slipped through the fence a couple of days ago and he'd spent the majority of the day before rounding them up. After moving them to the south pasture, he had been too tired to do anything else. It was times like these that he regretted his decision to help his brother out at the police station. He would never tell Creed, but working as a deputy, along with taking care of the ranch, was starting to take a toll on him. He was always exhausted now, but forced himself to push through daily.

After quickly putting his tools away, Ryder gathered up the reins and slipped them over Cochise's neck. Family always came first, he reminded himself as he swung up into the saddle. Without family, you had nothing. He would do what needed to be done for his, without complaining. Turning the Palomino toward the ranch, he let the horse set his own pace home.

Forty-five minutes later Ryder walked through the doors of the police station, a box of donuts in one hand and a tray with four coffees in the other. Grinning at the receptionist, Claire, he set the donuts down on the counter in front of her and removed one of the coffees. "Good morning, Miss Claire," he said in greeting, smiling widely when her pale cheeks blushed a pretty shade of pink. "I brought you breakfast." The girl was way too young for him, but there was nothing wrong with some harmless flirting. Besides, she was adorable with her long dark, blonde hair and wide, hazel eyes. Not only that, but he also enjoyed annoying the hell out of Cody when he was around because he knew the kid had a crush on her. Ryder chuckled softly when he saw a dark glare aimed his way from across the room. Yep, he had successfully managed to piss the deputy off.

"Thank you, Ryder," Claire responded shyly as she accepted the coffee. Shaking her head when he opened the donut box, she told him, "I already ate breakfast." Ryder frowned, but closed the box deciding not to press it. Recently Claire had begun losing weight rapidly. No one knew why, and she refused to discuss it. Ryder tried to get her to talk to him several times, but she would always immediately close up and turn back to her work.

Shrugging it off for now, he grinned, "That's okay, Claire. I'll eat yours too."

Claire giggled in response, but Ryder noticed the laughter didn't quite reach her eyes. "Creed and Katy are waiting for you in Creed's office," she told him, as she took a small sip of her hot beverage. "Thanks again for the coffee."

With one last look at her once again pale complexion, Ryder picked up the rest of the coffee and donuts and made his way to Creed's office. Kicking the door shut behind him, Ryder nodded to his brother and sister as he placed their breakfast on Creed's desk. "Dig in," he offered before grabbing a blueberry-filled donut and sinking his teeth into it, groaning as the sweet taste hit his tongue.

Katy laughed as she leaned forward in her chair to look into the large white box. "You do realize it's almost lunchtime, right?" Selecting a cherry-filled pastry, she moaned as she bit into it. "Sinfully Delicious has the best donuts, but don't you dare tell Dottie I said that!"

Ryder chuckled as he took another bite. Dottie was one of the waitresses over at Mac's Diner. They all loved to eat at Mac's place, but if you were looking for donuts or baked goods, Sinfully Delicious was the place to go.

Creed leaned forward and snatched one of the coffees out of the tray. Scowling, he took a drink before saying, "Take a seat, Ryder."

Raising an eyebrow, Ryder lowered himself into the other chair in front of Creed's desk and asked, "What has you all pissed off so early in the day?"

Katy's eyes sparkled with amusement as she quipped, "Sloane's out of town at a book signing in Arizona. He's probably a bit frustrated."

Shaking his head at them, Creed groused, "It has nothing to do with Sloane being gone. She was excited to meet some of her favorite authors and hang out with others she knows, and I'm glad she made the decision to go. Besides, she will be back tonight."

"Well then, what's wrong?" Reaching for her coffee, she closed her eyes, sighing in pleasure as she took a sip. "Are you having issues with the town council again?"

"No," Creed sighed heavily. "I almost wish I was."

Well, shit, Ryder thought as he finished off his donut and took a drink of his coffee. In the last few months, the people of Serenity Springs had been put through hell. It started with a crazy bastard stalking Sloane and then infiltrating the elementary school, endangering the lives of several children and almost killing one of the teachers. Then, just recently, another lunatic went after Lacey Donovan, the town coroner. He murdered two other local women before attempting to end his killing spree with her. What else could happen to their small town?

Deciding he wasn't ready for the answer to that question just yet, he grabbed a chocolate, cream-filled long john and took a bite before asking, "When does the new deputy arrive?"

"He's not coming," Creed said, running a hand through his thick, dark hair in frustration. "He decided small town living wasn't for him and accepted a position in Dallas instead. I'm sorry, Ryder. I know it has to be kicking your ass working the ranch and then having to patrol several days a week on top of it. I promise to get you out of here as soon as I can find a replacement."

"It's fine," Ryder replied, his hand tightening around the thick Styrofoam cup he held. If they really knew what he went through on a daily basis, they would be pissed that he didn't ask for help. But he wouldn't, that was just how he was. Ryder was the first to step forward and help anyone in need, but the last to ask for it for himself.

"What's really going on, Creed?" Katy asked quietly, leaning back in her chair and cradling her coffee cup with both hands. "Why are we in a closed door meeting? What has you looking so worried?"

Taking a closer look, Ryder realized his sister was right. Creed obviously was not happy, but something had him shook up as well. "Talk to us, brother," Ryder said, keeping his eyes trained on Creed.

Sighing deeply, Creed leaned forward, resting his forearms on the desk. "I got a call from an Assistant Director Talbot with the Federal Bureau of Investigation yesterday."

"Linc?" Katy whispered in fear. Creed had told Katy and his brothers about Linc's involvement with the FBI, but they were keeping it quiet from everyone else, including their parents. It was the only way to ensure their brother's safety.

"No," Creed replied, rubbing a hand over his face. "This has nothing to do with him." Ryder breathed a sigh of relief as Creed went on, "It seems one of their agents has purchased the Andrews place and will be moving in soon."

Katy cocked an eyebrow, a slow grin forming on her lips. "Does this agent need a job?"

A short burst of laughter slipped past Creed's lips. "I wish. I would give her one in a heartbeat. I can tell you, Rayna Williams has guts, that's for sure."

Rayna Williams. Ryder turned the name over in his mind. He liked it. It was both strong and sexy. He wondered what she looked like. Then Creed's words sank in. She was buying Olivia's old house.

The Andrews had purchased it after Olivia and her family died in a car accident just over twelve years ago. Olivia...his best friend. They were inseparable after she moved to Serenity Springs with her family in the third grade. Over time, Ryder's feelings grew stronger, and the night of their graduation he decided to tell her how he felt. That was the night of the accident. He never had the chance to tell her that he loved her. There was no funeral, so he never even got to tell her goodbye. There had been no closure on his end, and it had always haunted him.

"From what Talbot told me, Agent Williams is moving here to draw a known mob boss from D. C. out of hiding. He wouldn't give me very much information, but he told me he was sharing what he did as a common courtesy."

"Bullshit," Katy interrupted. "Since when does the FBI play nice with small town cops? He has an agenda." Katy was young, but she had more knowledge regarding law enforcement than others with twice her experience. She was very intelligent, and absorbed information like a sponge. "What did you tell him?"

"I told him I didn't want his agents in my town causing trouble. That we'd had enough of that over the past few months, and didn't need any more." Raking his hand through his hair once more, Creed admitted darkly, "By the end of the conversation, he had me eating out of his fucking hand. He made it clear that Rayna Williams was coming here no matter what any of us wanted, and we could either support her or ignore her. He promised to keep us informed on the situation and I told him he had our full support."

"Which was exactly what he wanted," Katy guessed. "He didn't call to play nice. He called because he wants help looking after his bait."

"This doesn't make sense to me," Ryder interjected, his brow furrowing in confusion. "Why would they place one of their agents here in Serenity Springs to draw a mob boss out? Wouldn't it be easier to do in his own city?"

"I have no idea," Creed replied, slamming his fist down on the desk. "All I know is that son of a bitch is sending his agent to my town and endangering my residents. And there isn't a damn thing I can do about it. He made that part perfectly clear."

"When is she supposed to arrive?" Katy asked quietly. Ryder could see wheels turning in her head, but he was afraid to ask what she was thinking. Hell, he was still trying to wrap his mind around the fact that someone new was moving into Olivia's house. It had broken his heart when the Andrews bought it just six months after the accident, because it made him face the fact that the Johnsons really were gone.

"I have no idea. It's all a waiting game on our end now."

"I'll keep an eye on the house," Ryder volunteered. The Johnson residence, that was how he would always think of the small farm, was just up the road from the Caldwell ranch. It would be easy for him to drive by a couple times a day to check on it.

"Hopefully Agent Williams will introduce herself when she comes to town," Creed drawled as he stood, "but it's a good idea to watch the old place just in case she doesn't show us the professional courtesy of a meeting."

"Maybe she will stay clear of the station so that she doesn't draw attention to herself," Ryder suggested, although he had a bad feeling the woman wasn't going to be worried about who saw her.

"From what I gather, the whole idea is to get this guy's attention. I don't think Rayna gives a shit who sees her." Placing his Stetson on his head, Creed motioned to the door. "Well, we can't just sit around and wait for the woman to arrive. We have jobs to do."

Ryder rose, tossing his empty coffee cup into the trash. "You're right. There's nothing we can do about Rayna Williams right now, but there might be something we can do for Claire. What's your take on her? She's still not eating, and I could tell something was bothering her this morning."

Katy's eyes narrowed in concern. "She's definitely not the happy young lady we hired a year ago. I've been watching her closely the past few days.

She's losing weight and the shadows under her eyes are becoming more pronounced. It might be stress related. I know she's taking a lot of college courses, along with holding down a full-time job."

"Why don't you try and talk to her this afternoon, Katy?" Creed suggested as he opened the door. "She might respond better to a female. If something is going on, if she needs help, I want to know."

Nodding, Katy stood and followed Creed out of the office. Ryder smothered a yawn as he followed. His day started way before dawn, and it was not even half over yet. He had his patrol shift first, then a pregnant mare to check on, horses to feed, stalls to clean, and he really needed to figure out what was wrong with the tractor he used to haul hay. He'd had a difficult time keeping the damn thing running lately.

Calling out a greeting to Jace Walker, the deputy he would be riding with that day, Ryder pushed down his exhaustion and grinned. "Let's go, Walker. I want to stop by Mac's and grab a bagel."

"You just ate two donuts," Katy groused, shaking her head in disgust.

"Yeah, but there's this cute little dark haired beauty at Mac's that Jace likes to drool over while I talk to Dottie. And since I'm in the giving mood today…"

Ryder laughed when Jace flipped him off, but in the back of his mind his thoughts were on Rayna

Williams. Why would someone volunteer for a mission like the one she was on? Did the woman have a death wish? How the hell were they going to keep her safe?

Chapter 6

After three full days of meetings, Rayna was finally allowed to leave for Serenity Springs. Agent Brentworth left the day before, driving an older Ford pickup truck, and hauling a horse trailer with a gorgeous Buckskin gelding in the back. At first she assumed the agency obtained the horse for him to go along with his undercover identity, but she'd been wrong. Pistols belonged to Nathan, and had for over five years. Rayna hadn't even recognized the man when she and Agent Donaldson stopped by a pre-arranged meeting place to go over everything one last time. His hair was now a light brown, his eyes pale blue with the help of contacts. Instead of his usual suit and tie, he wore a black tee-shirt that clung tightly to his thick, muscular chest. His jeans were frayed and well worn, with a rip in one knee. He'd tilted the brim of his dusty Stetson back with a cocky grin and drawled, "Hello beautiful. The name's Nate Burrows. I don't believe we've met?"

Rayna had almost swallowed her tongue. Gone was the gruff, straight-laced FBI agent. In his place stood a laid back, cocky-as-hell cowboy dripping of sensual recklessness. "You better tone that down some around those young teenagers," she warned, fighting laughter. "They are very impressionable at that age." Nate just shrugged, and continued on with the meeting, never once letting go of his new persona.

The agency decided not to go too in depth with a cover story for her. Everyone agreed sticking as close to the truth as possible was best. They had no idea how much information Diego Cortez had managed to dig up on her already from the mole in their office, and they didn't want to compromise the mission before it even started. Besides, the idea was to draw Cortez to her, so there was no reason to hide. Right now, Rayna's file stated that she was on an extended leave of absence for the next few months. She was taking a much needed break before starting a new position with the federal office in Dallas, Texas, which was closer to her new home in Serenity Springs. That position would not be available until after the first of the year, but it had already been promised to her.

The drive from Virginia to Texas took two days, but she had finally arrived. Entering Serenity Springs, Rayna pulled up to a four-way stop on the town square, taking a moment to look around briefly while she waited for her turn to continue on. It had been twelve years since she'd last been there, but the place still looked the same for the most part. She could see some new business establishments, but the building layouts on the outside were still the same. She smiled at a mother and small child who crossed the street in front of her, before taking her foot off the brake and slowly pulling through the intersection.

Even though she was tempted to, Rayna did not stop anywhere in town. Instead, she drove through and turned east onto Highway 2. After another mile, she turned south onto a rock road. Rayna knew she should check in with the sheriff, but she wasn't ready for that conversation just yet. First, she needed to go see the last place she had ever truly been happy. She needed to go home.

In just three more miles, Rayna found what she was looking for. Her hands trembled slightly as she turned right, and then slowly drove down the long driveway to the old farmhouse. It was a large, two story home with a beautiful wraparound porch. The house was freshly painted, a pretty yellow color with white trim, and she could just barely catch a glimpse of a white gazebo in the back. She remembered spending hours in that gazebo, curled up on the seat reading, and dreaming about a blond haired boy with mesmerizing blue eyes who made her pulse race, and a crooked grin she had wanted to trace with her fingertips. She'd never gotten the chance, but those dreams stayed with her for years.

Slowly making her way around the circular drive, Rayna's hands tightened on the steering wheel before she came to a stop in front of the house. She sat there for a long moment before finally shutting the car off and removing the key from the ignition.

Shoring up her courage, she made herself open her car door. As much as she wanted to be there, needed to be there, a part of her wished she could just start the car and drive right back down the driveway.

So many memories were rushing back at once. Memories she had managed to suppress for years. Matty chasing their dog, Bandit, across the yard, his loud giggles lost in the wind as they raced around. Her Mom hanging up laundry on the clothesline, a loving smile spread across her pretty face as she watched them run. Her sister had always been closer to their mother, while Rayna was a daddy's girl. She and her father were so much alike, from their love of books, to the way they enjoyed anything that had to do with the outdoors. There were many nights she, Matty, and their father would pitch a tent in the backyard and camp out, roasting marshmallows over a small fire, while her mother and sister stayed inside watching movies and eating popcorn.

To the right of the house was an older, dark red barn where Matty liked to play with his tractors on the dirt floor. Rayna preferred snuggling the cats and kittens that lived in the loft while daydreaming about anything and everything.

Rayna felt her chest tighten with suppressed emotions as she finally made herself get out of the car and walk to the house. When she found the place for sale online the month before, she bought the house sight unseen, without even bothering with any home inspections or a walk-through. She received a lot of money when her family was murdered; money that she had only used for college, preferring to get a job and pay her own way in life, and so she was able to purchase the home with cash. The paperwork was signed in front of a notary in Virginia, and the keys handed over at that time.

Forcing her legs to move, Rayna reluctantly climbed the stairs to the porch and made her way to the front door. Her breath caught in her throat when she swore she heard her mother's laughter and Bandit barking. She missed her family so much. Inserting the key into the lock, Rayna turned it, pushing the door open and stepping inside the entryway. To her right was a large, open living room with light-colored carpet and beige walls. Walking slowly through it, she smiled tremulously as she remembered sitting on an old, light blue couch beside her sister, listening to Ryder Caldwell strum his guitar as he sang to them. He always had his guitar with him back then, and she loved it.

Next was the dining room. There had been many family dinners at a large table in the middle of that room. So much teasing and laughter, and even some tears on occasion, but always love. They had all been so close.

Her heart breaking at the memories, Rayna turned and made her way across the room, before stopping in the doorway of a bright yellow kitchen.

There was a small table with four chairs under the window straight across from her. A breakfast nook separated the area from the kitchen appliances, and a laundry room was through a door in the back of the kitchen area, along with a small bathroom. She remembered her mother and sister baking cookies while she and her brother tried to steal them. Her mother always tried to get her to help make them, but Rayna would rather lick the batter from the bowl. She chuckled softly, thinking that she still wasn't much of a cook. She lived on takeout and TV dinners normally, which was just fine with her. Give her a gun over an oven any day.

After one last look around, Rayna made her way back through the large, empty house to the stairs leading up to the second floor. Trailing a hand lightly along the dark wood of the banister, she slowly climbed the stairs to the bedrooms above. When she reached the top, she turned to the right and walked toward a smaller room at the end of the hall. It was painted a light green color with white trim. When they lived there, it had been dark green with a John Deere border around the top. Matty used to spend hours in the middle of the floor playing with little cars, trucks, tractors, and trailers. Tomboy that she was, Rayna loved to play with him.

Fighting tears, Rayna turned and walked back down the hall, stopping in front of a large, open, cream-colored room. Entering it, Rayna let out a shaky breath, the tears now flowing freely down her cheeks. It was the bedroom she had shared with her sister. Crossing the room, she stopped by the large window with the cushioned bench beneath it. Placing a trembling hand on the wall to the side of the window, Rayna gazed out over the pasture land below. This had always been her favorite place in the house. If you could not find her in the gazebo or hayloft with a book in her hands, this was where she would be, lost in someone's fantasy. Books had been a way for her to dream about love and adventure, and forget about the reality of their lives; always living in fear that they would someday be found by Diego and his men.

She remembered clearly the way the room looked when she was growing up. The walls painted a light blue color, the border made up of magnificent horses. Rayna's side of the room held two bookshelves, both stuffed full of books she loved to get lost in. Her sister's side had its own shelves filled with captivating images she'd taken throughout the years. She loved taking pictures and watching them come alive when they were printed. She had dreamt of becoming a famous photographer someday, living in California or New York.

Squeezing her eyes shut tightly, Rayna rested her forehead against the wall as she recalled the whispered conversations she and her sister would have nightly; from their love of horses, to cute boys, to their hopes and dreams of the future. Only a year apart in age, they had been very close. There was one secret Rayna never shared with anyone, though, especially not her sister. She had never admitted her feelings for Ryder Caldwell to anyone except herself.

Taking a deep breath, Rayna pushed down the memories threatening to tear her apart. Wiping the wetness from her face, she left the room and made her way down the hall, pausing in front of the last room. The master bedroom where her parents used to sleep.

Entering the room, Rayna's gaze slowly wandered around the pale yellow room. She could picture her parents' king-sized bed on the far wall, large enough for Rayna and her siblings to crawl in and cuddle with their mother. They had spent several Saturday mornings in that bed watching cartoons when they were younger. They would laugh and giggle for hours over the silliest things.

Unable to stand the bittersweet memories any longer, Rayna dropped to her knees in the middle of the floor and sobbed. Grief swamped her and anger began to rise. Why had she lived when the rest of her family was taken from her? They were gone. All of them…gone. She had been alone for so long, facing all of life's trials and tribulations on her own. Unable to hold the pain deep inside any longer, Rayna felt a bellow of heartache and rage rip from her throat, scream after scream following.

Chapter 7

Ryder reined Cochise in as his gaze rested on the farmhouse before him. It had been years since he'd been this close to Olivia's old place. At first he had visited daily, hoping by some miracle that she and her family would return; that the news of their accident was a horrible mistake and they had just left suddenly for a surprise vacation or were visiting family somewhere, and would be home soon. Finally, when he was able to admit to himself that they would not be coming back, he decided avoiding the place was a better idea. After that, he only stopped by once a year, on the anniversary of their deaths, and he never allowed himself to get near enough to the house to be spotted trespassing by the new owners.

There was a black, four-door car parked in front of the house, the back filled with boxes. It looked like Rayna Williams was finally here. They were beginning to wonder if she'd changed her mind, which no one would blame her if she did. What she planned to do was just plain crazy in Ryder's opinion.

As he was debating on whether or not he should go knock on the door and introduce himself, a blood-curdling scream came from inside the house. After quickly calling for backup, Ryder urged Cochise across the large expanse of yard that separated him from the house at a dead run. Reining him in at the bottom of the porch steps, he swiftly dismounted. Pulling his gun from the holster at his side, Ryder raced up the stairs and didn't hesitate to push open the front door.

The screams were coming from the second level of the house. Not wasting time to clear the main floor, Ryder flew up the stairs and briefly checked the bedrooms to the right of the long hallway before swiftly making his way toward the other end. He stiffened when he looked into the last bedroom. There, kneeling in the middle of the floor, was a small woman who he assumed was Rayna. Her small hands were clenched tightly into fists at her sides. Her head was flung back as if she were yelling at the heavens, her dark brown hair resting just below her shoulders. The pain and anguish on her beautiful face twisted his insides, and when she screamed loudly again, he could not stop himself from stepping forward.

"Rayna," he crooned soothingly, cautiously making his way toward her. The woman's eyes sprang open and she quickly reached for her gun. "Hey now, sweetheart," he said with a gentle smile as he slipped his own gun back into his holster, "it's alright. I'm not here to hurt you."

As she continued to stare at him, he saw her eyes widen in shock. His own gaze narrowing, he felt his heart jump and then speed up erratically. This could not be happening. No fucking way was this happening. He blinked several times before swallowing hard and taking a step forward.

He would know those big, alluring brown eyes anywhere. He'd seen them so many times when he was growing up. Her hair had been longer, almost to her waist, and a shade or two lighter. She was older now, but her features were unmistakable; so much like her sister's, yet so different.

"Macey?" he rasped, as he fought to comprehend what was happening. Shaking his head in denial, Ryder took another step closer before whispering hoarsely, "I thought you were dead? They told us there was a car accident. That your whole family died."

Rayna slowly tucked her 9mm back into her holster as she stared at the man in front of her. A dusty, cream-colored straw Stetson covered short, blond hair. Dark lashes framed clear blue eyes that looked at her in stunned shock. He had a strong jawline, and a perfect mouth with hard lips that were slightly open as he watched her. Ryder was dressed in a blue and white sleeveless checkered shirt, tight Wranglers, and a pair of dirty cowboy boots that were clearly worn by a hardworking rancher. It was just the way she remembered him, for the most part. He was obviously older, and harder. His body had filled out into a long, lanky, and muscular build. She could see tattoos on each arm and one peeking out from his button-up shirt on his chest. Years ago, he didn't have tattoos. She loved body art, and wanted to see what else graced his skin.

She'd missed him so much. His teasing, his laughter, his music, everything about him. At least everything about the boy he used to be. She was sure there were things about him besides his appearance that had changed, just like there were things about her that were different now too.

"You're alive," he rasped again. "Does this mean…? Is Olivia?" And right there was the reason she had never told anyone how she really felt about Ryder Caldwell. Even at seventeen years old, she knew that Ryder didn't return her feelings, because those amazing, captivating eyes were always on her sister.

Taking a deep breath, Rayna placed her hands lightly on her hips. "Hello, Ryder," she said softly, unable to tear her gaze away from his.

Before she could respond to his question about Olivia, Rayna heard the sound of a car coming down the long driveway. Quickly moving past Ryder, she ran to Matty's old room to look out the window. She relaxed when she saw that it was the sheriff's truck. Rayna watched as Sheriff Creed Caldwell and

Deputy Katy Caldwell stepped out of the vehicle, their guns drawn and ready. It was nice to know she would have backup on this suicide mission, as long as no one got themselves killed.

Turning to leave the room, she stopped short when she saw Ryder blocking the doorway. He was leaning on the doorjamb, hands placed on either side of the door frame effectively blocking her escape. "Is she alive?" he demanded roughly.

Slowly, Rayna shook her head in regret. "No, Ryder. She's not. I'm the only one who survived that night. Trust me, I wish it were different. I would give anything to have my family back."

The muscle in his jaw ticked, but that was the only outward sign that he had heard her. His face became a mask, a blank slate showing no emotion, before he turned and walked away.

Rayna stood alone in the empty bedroom for several moments, before finally following him down the stairs and out the front door where he stood talking to his brother and sister. She waited silently on the porch at the top of the stairs for them to acknowledge her presence before saying, "Creed, Katy. I was going to come and check in at the station after my stop here." Gazing out over the yard and into the fields beyond, she went on, "I have a lot to tell all of you. We can do it here or at the station, but staying out in the open like this is not a good idea."

"Do you think Cortez already knows that you are here?" Creed asked, his voice low and gravelly.

"I wouldn't put it past him," Rayna replied, glancing back in his direction. "But even if he does, I don't think he will strike yet. He will watch, and he will wait until he thinks my guard is down, just like he did with my parents. Unfortunately for him, my guard will never be down. I worry more for you and your family's safety than my own."

"We are here to help you, Macey," Katy said as she stepped forward, her eyes full of concern and sympathy. "You don't have to go through this alone."

"It's Rayna now. I haven't been Macey Johnson since I woke up and found out that son of a bitch killed my entire family. After that, I became Rayna Williams, and I have fought hard every day to become the woman I am now. The woman who will take Diego Cortez down." And she would bring him down, there was no doubt in her mind. Her dark eyes glittering with determination, Rayna turned and walked back to the front door. Opening it, she looked back, "It's better if we have this discussion here at the house. I don't want to endanger any more people than I have to."

Walking through the screen door, Rayna let it slam shut behind her. If they wanted to hear her story, they would follow. Passing through the living room, she walked into the kitchen and took a seat at the table, her back against the wall. Whenever the

Andrews sold the house to her, they agreed to let her purchase the washer, dryer, kitchen appliances, and kitchen table. That was all she had in her home at the moment, but she was alright with that. She wouldn't be adding much more. She knew she could lose it all when Cortez's men showed up. Those bastards did not play nice, but then, neither would she.

Crossing her arms over her chest, Rayna leaned back in her chair and waited patiently for the Caldwells to enter the house. She knew it wouldn't take long. They wanted answers, and she was the only one who had them.

Creed led the way into the kitchen moments later, followed by Katy, and finally Ryder. Katy sat in the chair across from Rayna, Creed chose to lean against the breakfast bar, and Ryder stopped just inside the doorway, leaning his shoulder against the wood trim.

"You are the only one who survived the crash that night?" Katy questioned softly.

"Yes." Rayna fought against the tears that threatened again. Being back in her old home had her on edge, her emotions running wild. She missed her family so much. Talking about them was very difficult. Taking a deep breath, she forced herself to continue, "When I was a child, my father worked for an accounting company in D.C. One night, his boss asked him to stay late to help him figure out why there was a discrepancy in some figures for one of his clients. They were having a difficult time finding the issue, and Dad could tell his boss was becoming more and more agitated for some reason. When Mr. Herrington left the room for a few minutes, Dad took a closer look at the files and found out the client was actually Diego Cortez. Everyone in the D.C. area knows who Diego Cortez is." Glancing away from Katy, Rayna let her eyes fall first on Creed before moving to Ryder. "He is the head of the Mafia in D.C."

"Son of a bitch," Creed swore softly.

Turning back to him, Rayna nodded gravely. "When Mr. Herrington returned, Dad confronted him about it, asking him what in the hell he was doing working with a man like that. He was told to mind his own business and just find the discrepancy in the figures, or he could start looking for a new job." Shaking her head in frustration, Rayna ground out, "Dad didn't have a choice. He had to take care of his family. A couple of days later, he finally figured out what the problem was. One of the employees was skimming money off the company, and he was altering all of the files to throw anyone off who may find out and take a closer look into it. My father told his boss, but it was too late. What he did not know, was that not only did Aztec Accounting handle the accounts of Diego Cortez, but the company was actually owned by Cortez. So not only was that employee stealing money from the company, he was stealing from the mob. Cortez sent his men to deal with the problem two days later. They shot and killed both the employee who was caught stealing, and Mr. Herrington. Then they told my father that he was in charge now. They said he better make sure everything ran smoothly from then on, or he would follow them in death. My Dad was a good man. An honest man. He went straight to the FBI in Virginia and told them everything. They promised protection for him and his family if he would testify against Cortez, so he did. But, Cortez walked because he has people everywhere. He got off on a technicality because he had the judge in his pocket, and the jurors were terrified of him."

Creed swore again. "And then what happened?"

"Cortez promised my father after the trial that he would kill not only him, but his wife and children as well. He said he would not stop until all of us were dead. After that, the U.S. Marshals stepped in and relocated us to Serenity Springs." Letting a small smile escape, Rayna whispered, "Life was wonderful for so long after that." Rayna leaned forward, resting her arms on the table. Clasping her hands together, she looked at all of them. "My father was honest with us from the beginning about what happened because he wanted us to be alert to any danger at all times. We had escape routes planned out just in case anything was to happen. At first, we went over them two to three times a week. But, as time passed, we grew more lax. After a while, it was like Cortez just disappeared, and we moved on."

"But Cortez was just waiting, biding his time," Katy guessed.

"Yes," Rayna answered, nodding slightly in agreement. "The bastard waited until we formed new lives here in Serenity Springs, until we were so involved with our friends and everyday things that our thoughts of him were fleeting. I don't know how long it took him to find us. Hell, I don't even know how he did end up finding us. It could have been because my mother refused to change our first names." Shaking her head, she whispered, "She refused because she said that we needed some normalcy in our lives. So, even though she agreed to change our last name, all of our first names stayed the same. I believe that was part of our downfall. Also, I found out recently that there is a leak in the FBI. We haven't been able to track down the source yet, but we will."

"Why did you choose to come back here to fight this battle?" Ryder asked quietly. "Why not just take him out in D.C. on his own turf?"

Rayna rose and walked over to him. Stopping just in front of him, she responded softly, "For two reasons. First of all, he is too good to allow himself to be caught in D.C. He has always been a very patient man, and has no problem waiting until the perfect moment to take me out without getting caught. That moment won't come in D.C., but I am confident it will here." Her eyes narrowing, she continued, "And because I am going to end this once and for all. What better place to do it than where he took everything from me? That bastard destroyed my life, and now I'm going to destroy his." Glancing back at Creed and Katy, she said, "Now you know the whole story. Please, stay away and let me do my job. Cortez took my family from me. Please, don't let him take you too." Without another word, Rayna turned and walked away, leaving the house and the Caldwells behind. She needed to get some lunch, along with some provisions for the night, and she wanted to get the hell away from Ryder Caldwell and his family before she brought death to their door.

Chapter 8

"What do you think?" Katy asked quietly after Macey left the house. Not Macey, Ryder reminded himself, rubbing a hand tiredly over his face as he tried to process everything that she just told them. For all intents and purposes, Macey was gone. She was Rayna now.

"I think, no matter how you spin it, that woman is after revenge."

"She's after justice, Creed," Katy corrected. "Justice for her family who was taken from her way too soon, and justice for herself because she is the one who has to live with the fact that she is still here while they are all buried and gone."

"True," Ryder agreed. He saw the guilt that haunted her eyes when she talked about the death of her family. She was probably wondering why her life was spared, and somehow decided that it was so she could take down Cortez after everything he had done to her family.

"What do you think, Ryder?" Katy asked.

Ryder thought for a minute before responding. "I think, if it were me, I would hunt down not only Cortez, but every last one of his men, and show them just what happens when somebody fucks with my family. Because of that, I know that I am going to help Rayna, whether she wants me to, or not."

"Agreed," Katy said, rising from the table.

Creed removed his Stetson and raked a hand through his thick hair. "You both realize it could be years before Diego Cortez shows up here, if he does?"

Shaking her head, Katy replied confidently, "No, maybe months, but not years. There is no doubt in my mind that he will show, and he won't wait that long this time. Rayna challenged him by coming here. Not only that, but she has the FBI backing her. They have something planned, I can feel it. They wouldn't have agreed to let her come to Serenity Springs if they didn't. Cortez won't wait."

"Then we need to be ready," Creed cautioned, placing his hat back on his head. "We not only have a town to protect, but also an old friend. As tough as that woman may seem, there is no way she is going to take on the mob by herself and win."

"Well, he won't be here tonight, and I have animals to feed," Ryder grunted, turning to make his way through the dining room. The need to get out of that house and away from his siblings was almost strangling him. There was so much to think about, and the only good thing about any of it was the fact that Macey Johnson was alive. "I'll check on Rayna in the morning." Leaving the house, Ryder ran lightly down the steps and walked over to where Cochise still waited for him. Gathering up the reins, he swung easily into the saddle. Letting his gaze wander around the farm, his heart ached as he finally accepted the fact that Olivia was gone and she was never coming back. After twelve years of mourning his best friend, the girl he'd loved so many years ago, he could finally lay her to rest.

Taking a deep breath, Ryder turned Cochise toward home. He had the next couple of days off from the station, and there was so much work he needed to catch up on at the ranch. Urging the Palomino into a gallop, Ryder let his mind wander back to so many years ago, when he, Olivia, and Macey were just teenagers. Life was so much easier back then. He'd been the star quarterback on the Serenity Springs High School football team, Olivia the head cheerleader, and Macey…well, she had been all together something different; a good different, and someone he had mourned deeply as well.

Chapter 9

Rayna walked slowly around the town square, flooded with childhood memories. Even though a lot had changed in the small town since she'd lived there so many years ago, many things were still the same. Like the ice cream shop across from the hardware store where Rayna and her father used to stop when they were in town. They both had a sweet tooth, ice cream being their favorite way to satisfy it. They always ordered the same thing, a family sized banana split with no nuts, which they shared. Her dad let her have the three cherries on top, claiming he didn't care for them, but she knew that was not true. He ate them at home all of the time.

There was the appliance store that her friend's dad used to own. She'd come across his name in the obituary section of the town newspaper two years ago, and knew his wife had since sold the business and moved to Florida to be with her sister. Director Talbot would have been pissed if he found out Rayna subscribed to the Serenity Springs Tribune, but she didn't care. It was just one of the ways she'd been able to keep up on things in town. There was Mac's Diner, just a block off the square, where she and her family used to eat lunch after church almost every

Sunday. Serenity Springs was the only place that had ever truly felt like home to Rayna.

After confirming with the furniture store that her order was in and would be delivered later that afternoon, Rayna decided to grab a bite to eat at Mac's Diner before heading to the grocery store. Since she was not much of a cook, that trip wouldn't take long.

The bell on the top of the door jingled when Rayna opened it. She stepped inside, letting it shut gently behind her as her gaze wandered around the room. It was just as she remembered, from the bright red vinyl stools in front of a long counter, to the matching red booths. Old records decorated the wall behind the counter, and a jukebox stood in the back of the room. Rayna walked over to one of the empty booths, and slid in on one side. It didn't take long before a waitress appeared by her side. "Hello, sweetie," the woman said with a wide smile. "My name's Dottie. What can I get for you today?"

Rayna returned her smile, immediately liking the other woman's friendliness, and the open, honest expression on her face. Dottie's long, blonde hair hung in large curls down her back, her light blue eyes sparkled with happiness, and she looked as if she did not have a care in the world. *One of these days that will be me,* Rayna vowed. Once Cortez was out of the picture, she was going to learn how to live life to the fullest. Her smile grew when she realized that was the first time she thought of *when* she survived against the mob boss instead of *if*. "What's the special?" she asked, wondering if they still had one weekly like they used to.

"We have something new this month. Chicken barbeque nachos, and they are wonderful!" So it was monthly now instead of weekly. It probably made it easier to shop for food.

Before she could respond, there was a loud crash in the back of the building and someone started cursing loudly. "Oh, hon, I am so sorry. I will be right back!" Dottie promised, before rushing back into what Rayna assumed was the kitchen.

Hearing a child's laughter, Rayna turned to where a young mother sat with two small children. "No, Mama," the little girl giggled, "horses aren't purple!"

"No?" the mother teased, reaching over to pull on the child's braid. "What color are they?"

"Green!" the little boy piped up. The girl dissolved into a fit of giggles, shaking her head at him before picking up a brown colored card from the table and handing it to her mother.

Rayna turned from the family, a small smile on her lips. When her brother Matty was younger, he had colored everything green, it didn't matter what it was. It was his favorite color, so he used it on everything.

"I am so sorry about that," Dottie's words interrupted her thoughts. "We hired two new waitresses a couple of weeks ago, and one of them just needs a little more training is all."

Rayna hoped that it wasn't Lyssa that needed more training. They could not afford for her to be fired before their plans were even set into motion. "I'm sure she will catch on soon," was all she said.

"Of course she will," Dottie agreed with a chuckle, "she's just young, and this is her first job. At eighteen, everything is so scary, and Mac terrifies the hell out of her with his gruffness." So it wasn't Lyssa, that was good.

"Dottie, I think you might want to go back into the kitchen," a soft, female voice interrupted. "I will take this order."

Dottie's uncertain gaze went from the new waitress to Rayna, then back again. "She's crying, Dottie," the woman said quietly. "I think she is going to quit."

"Go," Rayna encouraged, "we will be fine."

After one last look at Rayna, Dottie apologized again before rushing back to the kitchen. "My name is Melissa. Sorry about the interruptions ma'am. Now, what can I get for you?"

Rayna took in the young woman in front of her. Just shy of twenty-eight years old, average height and slender, with short blonde hair and expressive light-blue eyes. This was Lyssa Taylor, or Melissa

Timmons as the town knew her. "I would love to try the special, please," Rayna told her, noticing how there was not one flicker of recognition in Lyssa's eyes. She was good.

"And to drink?"

"Diet coke, please."

Nodding, Lyssa wrote the order down on a notepad before saying, "I will have that out to you shortly."

Fifteen minutes later, Lyssa set a plate down in front of Rayna with a grin. "These are some of the best nachos you will ever have," she promised.

Thanking her, Rayna looked at the overflowing plate in front of her, her mouth watering in anticipation. It had been hours since she last stopped to eat, and her stomach was growling in protest. Glancing down, she noticed the corner of a piece of paper peeking out from under the plate. Looking around to make sure no one was watching, Rayna slipped the paper out and read it quickly. *Nothing new to report. Very quiet.* That was it, but it was enough to let Rayna know that as of right now, there was nothing to worry about.

After finishing her lunch, Rayna quickly paid and then left Mac's to continue her walk around the square. A moment later, her eyes fell on what used to be the used bookstore in town. Now it was called Turn the Page Bookstore. She knew that it was owned by Sloane Murphy, Creed's fiancée. She still sold used books, but from what Rayna had seen online, Turn The Page also featured new books by both traditionally published and self-published authors.

Deciding she needed something to help pass her time while she waited for Cortez to show, Rayna crossed the street, her eyes continuously scanning the area for anything or anyone who might look out of place. A bell clanged loudly when she opened the door and entered the warm, inviting room. The atmosphere inside immediately enveloped her, making her feel welcome. Stepping forward, she returned the smile of a woman standing at a counter in the front part of the store. Rayna had seen pictures of Sloane, but the bookstore owner was even more beautiful in person, with her long dark hair and pretty brown eyes. There was a huge stack of books in front of her and it looked like she was inputting the inventory into her computer.

"Good afternoon," Sloane greeted Rayna, immediately walking around the counter and offering her hand. "You must be Rayna Williams."

Rayna's eyes widened in surprise, but then she laughed. "Did you get that from small town living, or Creed?"

Sloane chuckled, her eyes lighting with mirth. "Maybe a little bit of both."

Rayna shook the other woman's hand as her gaze wandered around the large, spacious room. One wall was dedicated to new books, another to used.

Throughout the store were more used books on standalone shelves, and it looked like a children's reading area in the back. She could see everything from children's books, to young adult, to adult with a wide variety of different genres. But, what really interested her was the first half of the south wall.

Walking over to it, she grinned as she saw some of her favorite self-published authors' work showcased on their own separate shelves, the covers facing out to grab the attention of buyers.

"I've made several friends in the book world who publish on their own," Sloane commented, walking up behind her. "There are so many wonderful authors out there, both traditionally published and self-published."

"Yes," Rayna agreed, "there are." She grinned when her eyes alighted on a book by T.J. West. It was her new one, Lasting Lyric. Rayna had been waiting for it to come out. "Tiffany West is one of my favorite authors," she told Sloane as she picked up a copy. "I had never read rock stars until her series. Now I own all of her books in paperback, except this one."

Sloane grinned, "She's one of my favorites too. What other genres do you enjoy?"

"I normally prefer anything with suspense," Rayna replied absently as she continued to browse the shelves. "I love anything action-packed with some romance. There's a new author I've been wanting to try. She writes a thriller series. Hope is her first name."

"Hope Cavanaugh!" Sloane exclaimed, walking quickly back to the counter. "Hope is one of my good friends. I just got some of her books in today. She is absolutely amazing."

"I know there are three books out in that series. If you have them, I would like them all." She was going to have more than enough time to read them. Another book caught her eye as she turned to leave. It was a beautiful cover with a woman holding a camera, taking a picture. "Heather Dahlgren…have you ever read anything by her?" Rayna asked Sloane. It looked like it was the first book in the series, and there was one more out.

"I've read every book on that wall," Sloane responded as she opened another box of books, quickly unpacking them on the counter. "I have loved every one of them, and can personally recommend them all. Heather's Sexy series is my favorite series of hers."

Rayna picked up both books, scanning the back covers quickly, before adding them to her growing stack. Making her way to the front counter, she sat them down. "I will take both of these, and whatever you find of Hope's."

"I have the first three books in the series you were asking about. Now, these books aren't exactly romance books," Sloane advised as she handed them to Rayna to look at. "There is a small amount of romance in all of the books, but they are thrillers."

"That's perfect," Rayna grinned. "That's what I'm looking for."

Sloane laughed as she rang up Rayna's purchases. Adding some bookmarks with the books, she placed them in a teal bag sporting the bookstore logo and handed it to Rayna. "It was very nice to meet you, Rayna. I hope to see more of you."

Rayna paused for a moment, before setting her bag down on the counter with a sigh. She had lived her life full of lies and deceit. Running from a man who wanted nothing more than to kill her. She was done lying, and she didn't expect anyone else to lie for her, either. She had no idea how much Creed shared with Sloane, but this was one thing the man would not have to keep from her.

"Sloane," Rayna started slowly, pushing a lock of dark brown hair behind her ear. "I don't know how much you have been told about me, or my family, but I would like you to know who I really am. There is no reason for anyone else in Serenity Springs to be told at this time, but the Caldwells have always been good to me. I refuse to keep anything else from them."

Sloane reached over and covered Rayna's hand with her own. "You don't need to share anything with me, Rayna. We all have our secrets. I know that you are an FBI agent, and I know you are here putting your life on the line to capture a horrible man that deserves to be behind bars. You don't have to tell me anything else."

Rayna's eyes filled with tears as she looked into the compassionate, kind face of the woman in front of her. "Thank you for that," she whispered, "but I do need to tell you. I need you to understand why we can't be friends right now, even though I would love nothing more." Swallowing hard, she continued, "My real name is Macey Johnson. My family and I lived in a house near the Caldwell ranch when I was growing up. My sister was Ryder Caldwell's best friend."

Shock filled Sloane's eyes and her hand tightened on Rayna's. "Olivia," she murmured.

"Yes," Rayna replied, "Olivia. We were placed into the witness protection program when I was just a child. Diego Cortez, a mob boss out of the D.C. area, hunted us for years after my father discovered something he shouldn't have. He finally found us here, in Serenity Springs. Cortez killed everyone in my family, Sloane. Everyone. He took the people I loved from me. That is the man I am luring here. The man I am here to catch. And I refuse to bring that kind of danger to your door."

"Rayna," Sloane said softly, gently squeezing her hand, "you already have. Just coming here, to this town, you have endangered everyone who lives in it."

Rayna pulled away from Sloane, pain filling her as she acknowledged the other woman's words. She was right. Rayna had put everyone in Serenity Springs at risk the minute she stepped foot into the town. Unfortunately, she did not have a choice. There was no other way to capture Cortez. No other way to end this.

"And I apologize for that," she said as she once again picked up her bag. "It is not my intention to bring harm to you, or anyone else here. I just want this whole thing finished. I need to bring that man to justice for everything he did to me, to my family, and to every other victim out there. My superiors and I think coming here and drawing him out is the best way to handle this. Cortez will be coming after me, but as long as I am not close to any of you, he will just seek me out."

Turning to walk toward the door, Rayna paused as Sloane's soft voice reached her. "You can't do this alone, Rayna, and you don't have to."

"Yes," Rayna replied, opening the door before turning back to look at Sloane. "Yes, I do."

Chapter 10

Ryder swore softly when he scraped his knuckles against the engine of the old tractor. It was after 9p.m., and he had been working on the piece of shit for over two hours. No matter what he tried, the damn thing would not start. He knew he should just buy a new one. It wasn't that he couldn't afford it, he just preferred the old John Deere that had been his father's for years. Shaking his head in disgust, he wiped his bleeding hand on his jeans. There was one reason, and one reason only, that he could not figure out how to make the tractor run again right now. His mind was consumed with a pair of liquid brown eyes full of pain and despair one moment, and hard determination the next. Macey Johnson, Olivia's little sister, was back from the dead. Quiet, sweet, innocent Macey.

His young heart had yearned for Olivia's love, but there was a time before his feelings turned to more than friendship, when his eyes had strayed to her sister more than once.

Olivia had been the friendly, outgoing type; a cheerleader, a dancer, and prom queen senior year at their school. Macey was the quiet one, a dreamer, spending hours hiding somewhere with a book in her hands. She'd had a sweet, gentle soul back then. One that touched anyone she allowed to get close.

In the summer of their junior year, Olivia had taken part in a play put on by the local drama club. Ryder normally met her at her house after she was done with practice and he was done with his chores. One day, he finished earlier than normal. He had been afraid if he didn't get away from the ranch while he could, his father would put him to work doing something else, and he wouldn't get the chance to show Olivia the new song he was working on. So as soon as he could, he grabbed his guitar and ran.

Hoping Olivia was already done as well, he showed up a half an hour early. Instead of Olivia, he found Macey in the gazebo out behind the house. She clung to the book in her hands, tears falling from her large eyes, soft sobs escaping. He remembered that day like it was just yesterday. It was the day he began looking at Macey as more than just Olivia's little sister.

"Macey," Ryder whispered, sitting down beside her, "what's wrong?"

"She died," Macey cried, dropping the book on the bench before scrubbing at the wetness on her cheeks. "She's dead, Ryder."

"Who?" he asked, reaching out to run a hand gently down her long, soft hair. Liking the way it felt against his hand, he did it again.

Pointing at the book, she whispered, "Bailey. The girl in my book. She died. She had cancer and they couldn't save her. Why would they do that, Ryder? Why would they end a book like that? That's just horrible."

Ryder sat there unsure how to respond. It was just a book. No one was really dead. It was a piece of fiction…not real. What the hell was wrong with her? "I guess not everyone gets their happily ever after," he finally said with a shrug.

"But they should," Macey cried. "In all books, they should. I know it isn't true in real life, but she should have made it, Ryder. She should have lived."

Not knowing what else to do, Ryder enfolded Macey in his arms, pulling her close and holding her gently until her tears finally stopped. Eventually, she leaned back and looked at him. His heart clenched tightly, and he gulped. She was so pretty. Why hadn't he noticed that before? He could have drowned in the deep brown pools of her eyes. Ryder returned her gaze for several seconds before shaking himself. After slowly wiping away what was left of her tears, he picked up the guitar he'd set next to him, and lightly strummed a couple of chords. "How about a song?"

The smile first spread slowly across her lips, taking awhile to reach her eyes, but eventually it did. "Yes."

Ryder sat with Macey until Olivia arrived home, and then came back the next day, and the next, just to see her. He ended up spending every afternoon with Macey until the play ended. He'd never told Olivia about the time he shared with her sister, and as far as he knew, Macey didn't either. He had come to care for her a great deal in those weeks, but things changed when Olivia was back.

Ryder cursed again when he accidentally dropped the wrench to the ground. Resting his arm against the tractor, he dropped his forehead to it, sighing deeply. He would be lying if he said he regretted any of his time back then with Macey. He had cared for her a great deal. Macey was the first Johnson to touch his heart, even if her sister had held it in the end.

"Ryder?"

Ryder stiffened at the tentative sound of Sloane's voice. He did not want to talk to anyone right now. He just wanted to get the damn tractor fixed and move on to the next thing that needed to be done. Knowing Sloane would never leave until he acknowledged her presence, Ryder straightened and turned to look at her. "Hey, Sloane. I see that brother of mine let you out of his sight for a few minutes?" he teased. Anything to distract her from the real reason she was there. Ryder knew why she was standing just a few feet from him, a frown on her face. It had been hours since he'd left Rayna's house. More than enough time for Creed to tell Sloane what transpired. He was just surprised it had taken this long for her to show up.

"Actually, he and Cassie are both asleep." Sloane grinned mischievously, "I snuck out to come see you."

A burst of laughter fell from Ryder's lips as he leaned over to pick up the discarded wrench. "Don't let him find out you went to see another man."

She walked over to climb up on the tractor and sit on the hard metal seat, before returning his laughter. "I won't tell if you don't."

"You got it."

Just as suddenly as it was there, the laughter was gone, and concern filled Sloane's gaze. "I met Macey today," she said quietly. "She stopped in the store this afternoon to purchase some books."

"Rayna," Ryder corrected, turning to work on the tractor again. "She goes by Rayna now."

"Yes, that's what she said."

"It fits her." Ryder grunted as he struggled with a bolt. "It's a strong, courageous name, and the woman is obviously full of either courage or stupidity. I'm not sure which one just yet." He knew. Rayna had always been a bright girl, at the top of her class. The woman had brains, but that didn't mean she was thinking clearly right now. She was out to get herself killed. He may respect the fact that she was taking a stand, but the issue he had was that she refused to ask for help. Too bad, she was getting it anyway.

"I like her," Sloane said, leaning toward him over the tractor wheel. "I think she's very brave. I wish I was more like her."

"You're perfect the way you are, little sis," Ryder grunted, pressing down harder on the wrench and finally loosening the bolt he'd been fighting with for the past few minutes. "Not everyone is meant to carry a gun and shoot at bad guys." Ryder faltered, once again dropping the wrench to the ground when he realized that chasing bad guys was exactly what Rayna did for a living. He'd never actually considered it before, but now that the thought had entered his mind, he could not push it out. Little Macey Johnson carried a gun. Not only did she carry a gun, but he would bet his last dollar that she'd used it in the line of duty. Hell, why did the idea of what Rayna did for a living bother him so much? The woman had the fucking mafia on her tail. She worked for the FBI, and would have had to have made her way up to the position she held now with them. She could handle herself, but he still could not shake the nagging worry. What if she got herself killed?

"Do you think Rayna is?" Sloane asked softly.

Retrieving the wrench, Ryder walked over and put it in his tool box. Shutting the top lid, he locked up his tools and turned to face Sloane. "In the past, I would have said no. Macey was a timid, sweet, innocent girl. But the person she has become? Rayna Williams?" Shaking his head, he said, "Rayna doesn't seem to be any of those things. She is strong, determined, and confident. She's worked hard to get where she's at, and if the FBI is trusting her with a mission like this, then she has to be damn good at what she does."

"I hope so," Sloane whispered. "I can't imagine being in her shoes right now. Knowing the mob is after you. That's just crazy! It's like something out of a movie. Things like that just don't happen in the real world."

"They do in Rayna's world," Ryder muttered, shoving a hand roughly through his hair. "It sounds like that is all she has known for a long time."

Sloane watched him for a moment before asking, "How are you, Ryder?" Holding up a hand before he could respond, she said, "I mean how are you really? Don't tell me that you are fine, because we both know that you aren't." Lowering her voice, Sloane murmured, "Macey is here…but Olivia isn't. That has to hurt, Ryder. Talk to me, please."

Ryder blinked back tears of sorrow and rage. They wouldn't do any good now. He had cried for Olivia and her family years ago, and now he just wanted to leave the past where it belonged. In the past. Resisting the urge to put his fist through a wall, he turned from Sloane and stared out the barn door into the night. "I don't know what you want me to say, Sloane. Do I wish Olivia was alive? Yes, of course I do. A part of me will always love her. But what we could have had together ended before it even started. She's gone, and there isn't a damn thing I can do about it." Looking back at her, he went on, "So, instead of dwelling on what can never be, I choose to look forward. Olivia may not be here, but her sister is. Rayna has come home, and even though the stubborn woman refuses to admit it, she needs our help."

Sloane slid down from the tractor and stood in front of him. "She isn't going to let any of us get close to her right now, Ryder. She is too worried that we will get hurt if she does."

"Well, she isn't going to have a choice," Ryder vowed. "I am not going to just let that bastard roll into our town and take her out."

Reaching out, Sloane gently laid a hand on his arm. "None of us are."

Chapter 11

It had been two long weeks since Rayna arrived in Serenity Springs, and things were still quiet. She had stopped in Mac's Diner three times the week before, and twice this week so far, but the news was always the same. *Nothing to report.* She hadn't heard from Nate at all, but he was scheduled to check in that Friday.

After she unpacked the few things she brought with her, and the furniture was delivered and assembled, there wasn't much else for Rayna to do. She went on daily runs, lifted weights she'd purchased that were now set up in her basement, and did regular outdoor target practice. She needed to stay in shape and be prepared for anything. She also spent hours reading, the only real pleasure she allowed herself.

Rayna was on one of her early morning runs, and wondering how long it would take Cortez to send someone after her. Even though she was willing to wait months if that was what it took, she was not as patient as she knew the mob boss could be. She just wanted the whole thing over with, no matter what the outcome was.

Turning down her driveway, Rayna opened up into a full on sprint the rest of the way to the house, pushing herself until she made it to the front porch. Gasping for breath, she wiped the sweat from her brow with her tank top and leaned over to stretch. All the while, she was extremely aware of her surroundings, so it was no surprise to her when a vehicle pulled into her driveway, making its way slowly down the lane, before coming to a stop beside her car. What did surprise her was the person who got out of the truck.

"Ryder," she said, straightening to greet him. "What can I do for you?"

She cringed when he took her in, head to toe, knowing she was one hot, sweaty mess. She'd just finished running five miles in the early August heat. Not that she should care what he thought about the way she looked…but for some reason she still did. No matter how hard she tried, she could not forget the boy from her past, or the feelings she still had for him.

"I haven't seen you since you moved in," Ryder responded casually, as he walked towards her. "I was on my way to work, and decided to stop by to see how things are going."

Raising an eyebrow, Rayna quipped, "That isn't you who has been watching me morning and night? Is there some other cowboy roaming around my land on a gorgeous palomino?"

Looking sheepish for just the slightest moment, Ryder shrugged, "I was just checking to see if you were still around. I wanted to make sure you are okay."

"Well, I am."

Ryder took a step closer, before stopping and resting his hands lightly on his hips. "We aren't going to just leave you alone, Rayna, no matter what you think."

"It's what I want," she insisted.

"I don't care," Ryder shot back. "It isn't what is going to happen."

Sighing, Rayna sat down on her front steps. "Ryder, no matter what, my life is in danger. If I am here, if I'm in Virginia, that isn't going to change. But it doesn't mean that yours has to be too, or that your family's does."

Ryder walked over and sat beside her, reaching out hesitantly to tuck a stray hair behind her ear. "I don't know how to stand down when someone I care about is in trouble," he admitted.

Shaking her head in confusion, Rayna whispered, "You can't care about me. You don't even know me anymore, Ryder. The girl that you used to know, the one you were friends with back then, she's gone. There isn't anything left of her. She died in that crash with the rest of her family."

"Then let me get to know you. Show me who you are now, who Rayna Williams is."

Sorrow flooded her heart as she looked into his intense blue eyes. He would never know how much she wished she could do that. She wanted nothing more than to spend time with the man beside her. He was all that was left of the people she loved from her past. Shaking her head, she murmured, "I'm sorry, I just can't."

Ryder watched her closely, before finally rising slowly to his feet. "It's okay," he said quietly. "I already knew that would be your answer." Gazing out over her land, he asked, "Have you talked to your colleagues in Virginia? Do they know if Cortez has eyes on you here yet?"

"Not yet," Rayna admitted. "I will contact them soon, but as far as I know, he hasn't taken the bait yet."

Nodding, Ryder took one last look at her before walking away. She sighed as she watched him get into his pickup and drive away without a backward glance.

Chapter 12

Ryder sat at his mother's kitchen table, surrounded by family, but not hearing a word that was being said. His thoughts were centered on the beautiful, courageous woman just a couple of miles from the Caldwell ranch, who refused to give any of them the time of day. He had been pissed when she turned him away that morning, but if he were honest with himself, he knew he would have done the same thing if he were in her shoes. He would alienate everyone he loved, or cared about, so that they didn't end up in a body bag after the mob arrived in town.

He fought back a groan as he remembered the way pieces of hair had escaped Rayna's ponytail, and how her eyes darkened slightly when he brushed it away from her face, accidentally skimming her cheekbone with his fingertips. Her hair was so soft, her skin so smooth.

Ryder jumped when a foot connected with his ankle under the table, glaring at his sister when she burst into laughter. "What the hell did you do that for?"

Katy raised an eyebrow, cocking her head to the side as a slow, somewhat evil grin spread across her face. "You haven't heard a word I've said."

"Yes I have," Ryder argued.

"Really?"

Shit, no he hadn't. Shaking his head, he returned her grin with a sheepish one of his own. "No, I haven't."

He was ready for his brothers to rib him next, and was surprised when all Creed said was, "You may want to start paying attention, Ryder. Your little sister has a hair-brained idea that she wants to leave us."

His eyes narrowing, Ryder looked over at Katy, "Leave? Where would you go?"

Katy shrugged, her face flushing a dark red. Ryder could not remember the last time he'd seen his sister look so uncomfortable.

"Katy," Caiden said quietly, "we are all for you following your dreams, wherever they may lead, but I thought your dreams were here, in Serenity Springs?"

"I thought so too," Katy replied softly, "but I just can't stop wondering.."

"Wondering what?" Ryder asked, afraid he already knew the answer. When Sloane moved in with Creed and his daughter Cassie a few months ago, Katy rented out her apartment above the bookstore. She said she needed to spread her wings, and get her own place, away from the ranch. He was beginning to see that it was so much more.

"Where I'm from," Katy finally admitted, "who I am."

"You are a Caldwell, child," his mother told her, reaching over to cover Katy's hand with her own. "You will always be a Caldwell."

"I know," Katy whispered, her eyes filling with tears. "I do know that, Mama, but sometimes I just feel empty, like something is missing."

"Let me finish," Cara interjected. "You are my daughter, and always will be, no matter what happens. I love all of you children more than life itself, but your father and I knew this day would come. We have been preparing for it since we found you at the orphanage." Wiping away the tears that slipped from Katy's eyes, she went on, "We promised ourselves the day we brought all of you home, that when it was time, we would support you when you were ready to find your birth parents. And we will. It would be selfish of us not to."

Ryder watched as his sister sank into his mom's embrace, clinging to her tightly. "Thank you," Katy said hoarsely, "thank you for understanding. It isn't that I don't love you. You will always be my parents. I just *need* to know where I'm from."

"We do understand, Katy," his father's voice was gruff, and Ryder swore he saw tears in the man's eyes too. "We will help you, baby girl, with whatever you need."

"What's the plan?" Creed asked.

Ryder stood, taking his empty plate over to the sink. Rinsing it off, he listened as his sister told them about a private detective she'd hired in April to find her birth mother. According to him, he was unable to find anything, and had no leads for her. Katy didn't believe him. She was going to go to the orphanage in Nevada and start there. "I won't leave until you find someone to take my place at the station, Creed," she promised, "or until we know Rayna is safe."

"Rayna will be fine," Ryder told them, walking to the door and grabbing his Stetson from where it hung on the wall beside it. "Go do what you gotta do. I can take on more hours at the station."

"No you can't, Ryder. You are already stretched too thin as it is." Creed's tone brooked no argument, but Ryder ignored him.

"It will work out," was all he said before walking out the door. He needed to get out of there. Family was everything to him, and now not only were both Linc and Justice gone, but his baby sister was leaving too.

Rayna sat on the reclining loveseat, her legs up, a paperback by Hope Cavanaugh on her lap, and her 9mm resting on the cushion beside her. The chocolate brown loveseat was the only piece of furniture in her living room, and it was a good thing it was comfortable, because it was also where she spent every night. She purchased a bedroom set with a king-sized bed when she moved in that was now upstairs in her old room, but refused to allow herself the luxury of actually sleeping in it. If she slept too soundly, she wouldn't hear anyone if they tried to break into the house. Not only that, but she was afraid the memories in that room would be too much for her right now.

The sound of a vehicle pulling into her driveway shook Rayna from her thoughts, and she clicked the mute button on the remote to quiet the television quickly, without actually turning it off. If the person coming down the drive saw it go off, they would know she was on to them before she could find out who it was. She was pretty sure Diego's men would not just drive in and knock on her door looking for her, but it was better to be safe than sorry.

Picking up her gun, Rayna slipped from the sofa, crouching down and moving swiftly across the floor. When she reached the corner window, she squatted in front of it, her eyes peering out into the darkness just over the windowsill. When the outside light illuminated a truck with the Caldwell Ranch logo on the side as it made its way around the front circle, she took a deep breath, lowering the gun and rising to go unlock the front door. Not waiting for his knock, she opened the door and found herself staring into eyes full of confusion and pain.

"Ryder," Rayna said quietly, stepping aside to let him in. She had no idea what was wrong with him, or why he was there, but there was no way she could turn him away.

Ryder walked in, stopping just inside the entrance to the living room. "Love what you've done to the place," he joked with an empty chuckle.

"Thanks," she responded lightly, shutting the door and locking it. "I like it." Rayna watched him silently, waiting for him to speak again. When he didn't, she said his name softly.

Ryder turned back towards her, removing his Stetson and running a hand through his short hair. He looked exhausted, like he held the weight of the world on his shoulders. "Since you already know that I have been checking on you throughout the day, I thought I might as well just stop by and see you this time."

Rayna knew there was more to it, but she decided to let him off the hook for now. "Well, you came just in time," she said with a smile. "There's a movie coming on soon that I've been wanting to see for awhile, and I have ice cream in the freezer calling my name." Nodding towards the loveseat she told him, "Why don't you have a seat, and I'll be back in a few minutes."

"You're going to let me stay?" he asked in confusion.

"You seem to need some company right now, Ryder, and as much as I hate to admit it, I could use some myself." She had no idea why she was letting him stay. Maybe it was the fact that she had been alone for two weeks straight, or that he looked like he'd just lost his best friend…or that she just wanted him near right now. Whatever it was, she was going to ignore the fact that she was going against her own rules about allowing someone to get too close, and let him stay for a couple of hours. "Just until the movie is over," she said, pointing a finger at him to emphasize her point, "then you go home, and I go to bed."

"Deal," Ryder agreed, dropping down into the loveseat, and leaning back in the recliner. When she turned to walk away, she heard him whisper, "Thanks Rayna."

Smiling to herself, Rayna made her way to the kitchen to get the ice cream, returning a few minutes later with two bowls full of chocolate and peanut butter cups, with chocolate syrup and whip cream on top. She stopped short when she saw Ryder, asleep on the sofa with his Stetson resting beside him. After taking the ice cream back into the kitchen, she returned and covered him with her blanket. Letting her gaze wander over his tired features, she resisted the urge to reach out and trace them with her fingers. He was all that she remembered, and so much more.

Taking one last look at him, Rayna stepped back with a sigh. It looked like she was going to be sleeping in her old room for the first time since she moved back, whether she was ready to or not, because there was no way she was going to sit beside Ryder when her emotions were running wild. She would probably end up doing something they would both regret.

Chapter 13

Ryder raised his arms above his head and stretched, trying to get the kinks out of his back. What the hell? He felt like he'd slept in the back of the truck instead of in his own bed. Grunting, he twisted his upper body, cursing out loud when his hand smacked against something hard. His eyes sprang open quickly, and he looked around, trying to figure out where he was. It took a full thirty seconds for his foggy brain to register that he was in Rayna Williams's living room, and another thirty to realize that he had missed out on his chance to have a couple of hours alone with her the night before when he passed out on her couch like a fool.

Raking a hand through his messed up hair, he muttered to himself, "You finally get her to spend time with you, and you pass the fuck out. Way to go, dumbass." A small grin appeared as he ran a hand over the light blue comforter that covered him. She must care a little if she'd taken the time to tuck him in before going to bed herself.

Glancing around, wondering where Rayna was, Ryder put the recliner down and stood up. He was stretching again when his phone vibrated in his pocket. Retrieving it, he grimaced when he saw his sister's name flash across the screen. Shit, he did not need this right now. Barely resisting the urge to ignore the call and turn his phone off, he answered, "Ryder." Katy was stubborn, persistent, and a huge pain in the ass sometimes, but he loved her.

"Where are you?" she asked, wasting no time with pleasantries.

That was a loaded question, he thought, wondering how he should respond. What did he tell her? He'd shown up at Rayna's last night because he was fucked up about another one of his family members leaving, and he didn't know where else to go? He couldn't tell his baby sister that. As much as he hated the idea of her leaving, he would never stand in her way.

"Ryder? Are you okay? You're late for work. You are never late."

His brow furrowing, Ryder pulled the phone back to look at the time. Shit, it was after 10 in the morning. He never slept past 6 o'clock, there was too much to do. He needed to feed the cattle, check on his pregnant mare, change, and get to work. He should have been there an hour ago. Closing his eyes tightly, he answered, "I'm going to be a little late this morning, Katy. I have a few things I need to finish up at the ranch, and then I will be there. Cover for me?"

After a moment, Katy murmured, "Of course, just get your ass in here." There was a pause, and then, "You would tell me if something was wrong, wouldn't you?"

No, he wouldn't. He hardly ever shared his true feelings with anyone. He liked to keep things close and private, even from his family. He never let them know that, of course. He hid behind jokes and a flirtatious attitude, showing only love and laughter on the outside. His problems were his own.

"I have to go, sis. I'll be there as soon as I can," was all he said before ending the call. Shoving the phone back into his pocket, he walked quickly through the dining room and kitchen to get to the bathroom in the back of the house. He needed to get to work, and there was so much to do before that could happen.

Making quick use of the facilities, Ryder went back to the living room, grabbed his Stetson off the loveseat, and headed to the front door. His mind on his jacked up morning, he almost missed the soft cry that came from upstairs. His hand on the doorknob, he turned toward the noise, stiffening when it came again, louder this time. *Rayna.*

Taking the steps two at a time, he rushed down the hall until he stopped in front of Olivia and Macey's old bedroom. Rayna lay in the middle of a large bed, thrashing back and forth. Her body was covered in a layer of sweat, a look of fear etched into her face.

"No," she moaned, "no. Please, no!"

"Rayna, it's okay," Ryder said, moving quickly across the room. Two seconds later, he was slowly stepping back, his hands raised in the air, held out away from him in a non-threatening manner. She held a gun leveled on him, her eyes glossed over, arms stiff and unyielding. "Rayna, it's me, Ryder." When she didn't respond, he stated more forcibly, "Put the gun down, Rayna. I am not going to hurt you." She was breathing heavily, the terror of her nightmare still clinging to her, but the hand holding the gun never wavered.

"Rayna, look at me," Ryder ordered, his hand held out to her in a placating manner. "Look at me. You are safe. It's just me. Ryder. I would never hurt you."

Slowly recognition crossed her face, and then a look of horror entered her eyes when she realized what was happening. "Ryder," she rasped, dropping the gun on the bed in front of her. Her hands covering her mouth, she whispered, "What have I done?"

Ryder closed the distance between them, picking up the gun and placing it on the bedside table. "Rayna, it's okay. You didn't hurt me."

Oh my God, what the hell was wrong with her? This was one of the main reasons why she didn't allow anyone to get close to her, and she *never* let anyone spend the night. She had no control over anything when she was under the spell of one of her dreams. It had happened one other time, six years ago, and although she didn't pull a gun on him, the guy did leave with more than one bruise shortly after she managed to break free of the night terror and fight her way back to reality.

She almost shot Ryder, believing he was someone else. The one person whose memory she had clung to all of these years. The person who helped her get through everything in her past and press on, even though he wasn't there and had no idea the affect their relationship as teenagers, and what she'd hoped at the time would turn into so much more, had on her.

"You're okay."

Rayna just shook her head. *What had she done?* Her life was so fucked up. Everything about her was fucked up. She would never be able to fall in love, never be able to spend the rest of her life with a man who loved her in return. Who would want to be with her? Someone who could kill them in their sleep without realizing what she'd done?

"Rayna," The deep sound of his voice interrupted her thoughts, "stop it, now."

She looked at him, tears slipping from her eyes and falling down her cheeks. "You need to leave, Ryder."

"I'm not going anywhere."

"Ryder, please," she almost begged, "I almost shot you."

"You are not going to hurt me," he responded gruffly, sitting down on the side of the bed beside her, "and I'm not going anywhere."

God, he had no idea what those words meant to her. She could not remember the last time someone wanted to be there for her, especially after what just happened. "I could have killed you, Ryder. I could have…"

"You didn't," he said, moving closer to her, "you didn't, and I don't believe that you ever could, no matter what you might think." Cupping her cheeks gently in his hands, he lightly rubbed the tears from her skin. "You would never hurt me, Rayna."

"Not on purpose," she whispered.

"Never," he insisted.

She wanted to believe him. Staring into eyes full of trust and conviction, she really wanted to believe what he said was true. But how could he be so sure, when she didn't even know herself what she was capable of?

Shaking her head, Rayna stiffened her shoulders. "You better go," she told him, even though all she wanted to do was close the distance between them and rest her head on his shoulder. To let someone else fight her demons for a day. Closing her eyes, she whispered again, "Go."

Her breath caught, a shiver running down her spine, when she felt Ryder's lips skim across hers briefly before he rested his forehead lightly against hers. “I’ll go for now,” he finally agreed, “but this isn’t over, sweetheart.” His lips lightly touched hers again, and before she could protest, he was gone.

Chapter 14

An hour later, Ryder walked into the station, consumed with thoughts of Rayna and the hell she must live through on a daily basis. He could not imagine spending every minute of the day knowing the mob was gunning for you. That it was a very real possibility you weren't going to wake up the next morning. Rayna's eyes had held so much pain and suffering that morning after she realized what happened, and then she built up a wall between them, trying to push him away. Huffing softly to himself, he muttered, "That wouldn't take much." She held them all at a distance, refusing to even talk to them if she saw them in town.

"I'm sorry, Ryder, did you say something?"

Ryder looked over at Claire, a grin on his lips to hide the emotions he felt inside, but came to a stop in front of her desk when he saw the vague, almost vacant look in her eyes. Ignoring his brother when Creed bellowed his name from Katy's office, Ryder rested his arms on the counter and leaned in to ask softly, "What's wrong, Claire Bear?" Claire turned her gaze up to meet his, but did not respond. "Claire, talk to me," he insisted. "Something is obviously going on with you. I want to help."

Claire slowly shook her head and looked back down at the paperwork in front of her. “There’s nothing you can do, Ryder,” she whispered, “but thank you.”

That was two women in the same day who thought that he was not man enough to help them out with their troubles. He obviously needed to work harder at portraying himself as a badass. He could wrangle a 2400 pound bull, carried a gun, and was ex-special forces, for fuck’s sake. What more did they want?

Leaning in closer, he drawled, “In case it slipped your attention, beautiful, I’m the law around these parts. I can do pretty much anything I want.”

For the first time in weeks, the pale, frail girl in front of him laughed, a real laugh that actually reached her eyes, and he saw a small piece of the old Claire surface. Unfortunately, before he could say anything else, Creed was at his side. “Nice of you to show up for work today,” he snapped.

Ryder gave Claire one last grin, tipping his hat to her, before he turned and walked out the front door. He made it to his truck before a stunned Creed caught up to him. “Ryder, where the hell do you think you are going? We are shorthanded here. I need you to get your ass back in that building now!”

Ryder took a deep breath before turning around to face his older brother. “If you want my help, then treat me like a human being instead of a piece of shit."

Creed's eyes narrowed, "Dammit, Ryder, stop acting like a two year old."

"I don't know what your problem is, Creed, but after the morning I've had…"

Creed snorted, "You mean after waking up with the hot piece of ass next door?"

Ryder's fist shot out, connecting squarely with Creed's jaw, and he barely ducked in time to avoid the swing that came back at him. "You have no clue what the fuck you are talking about," he snarled. There was no way he was going to let his brother talk about Rayna like she was trash. She was so much better than that.

Grunting when one of Creed's fists connected with his gut, Ryder stepped back to avoid the next jab.

"What the hell is wrong with the two of you?" Katy demanded, showing up and quickly inserting herself between them. "Stop this, now! The town doesn't need to see you two acting like fools."

Ryder fought the urge to move her out of the way, wanting the fight. Needing it to let out all of the aggression he had pent up over the last few months.

"Ryder?" Her voice came from behind him; strong, capable, and sexy as hell. His eyes never leaving Creed's, just in case his brother decided the fight wasn't over, he responded, "Hey, Rayna. How long have you been there?"

"Long enough to know that I'm hot," she quipped. "I saw your truck, and was coming over to apologize again for almost putting a bullet in you this morning, when your little party started."

Anger filled him again when he realized she'd heard their conversation. "Well, the party's over." Turning his back on Creed, he allowed himself to drink in the sight of the gorgeous woman in front of him. "Want some lunch?"

"Wait a minute," Creed ordered roughly, "what do you mean you almost put a bullet in Ryder this morning?"

When Rayna would have responded, Ryder shook his head. "It was nothing."

"It was obviously something," Katy said, concern in her voice.

Sighing, Ryder looked over at his sister. Knowing she would not stop until she knew the truth, he shrugged, "Not really, sis. I went to hang out with Rayna last night, and ended up crashing on her couch. She had a nightmare this morning that I was stupid enough to interrupt. End of story."

"Ryder…"

Reaching out, he took hold of Rayna's hand and laced their fingers together. "End…of…story," he said slowly and deliberately, looking Creed in the eyes. "Come on, Rayna, it's lunchtime, and I missed breakfast."

Rayna hesitated before following him down the street to Mac's Diner. "Your brother looks really pissed," she finally said, gently untangling her fingers with his.

Ryder shrugged, "He always looks like that." Rayna raised an eyebrow, but did not press him.

When they reached the diner, Ryder held the door open for her, and then followed behind her, waving to some of the local ranchers who ate lunch there several days a week.

Motioning to an empty booth in the back, Ryder walked up to the front counter and grinned at Dottie. "Hey there, darlin'," he said with a wink, "I don't care what I have for lunch, but I definitely want some of the apple pie for dessert."

Dottie cocked her hip, placing a hand on it, and raised both eyebrows. "After the show you and your brother just put on out in front of the station, you must be starving."

"Awe, Ma'am, you know how brothers can be," he grinned. "Those were just little love taps." There was no way Dottie saw the fight from inside the diner, but Serenity Springs was a small town. It didn't take long for news to spread like wildfire.

"Love taps," Dottie huffed, shaking her head at him even as a small grin appeared. "I'm glad my sister and I never shared any of those love taps when we were growing up."

"Who's the pretty little thing you are with?" Garrett Thompson asked, setting his cup of coffee down in front of him. "I wouldn't mind buying her dinner."

Ryder chuckled, "Good luck with that."

Walking back to where Rayna sat waiting, Ryder removed his hat and hung it on the wall next to the booth, before taking a seat across from her. "What would you like for lunch?"

"Look, Ryder…" the way she paused, Ryder figured she was going to tell him that she needed to leave. Instead, what he heard was, "I don't have many friends. Actually, I don't have any friends at all." Folding her hands on the table in front of her, she went on, "That's by choice. Diego will kill anyone and everyone he thinks I'm close to. Not only that, but being around me is dangerous for other reasons as well, which you learned this morning."

"I'm not afraid of Cortez," he said softly, "and I am definitely not afraid of you."

"Maybe not," Rayna whispered, "but if something were to happen to you, I would never forgive myself."

Ryder covered her hands with one of his. "Why don't you let me worry about that?" There was something about this woman, so stubborn and intense, willing to die to bring a man to justice, but not willing to allow others to stand beside her against that man.

"Can I take your order?"

Ryder held in his laughter when Rayna yanked her hands back, a dark blush staining her cheeks. Glancing at the pretty blonde in front of them, he grinned, "I'll take the special, please."

"Sure," she said, returning his smile. "And for you, Rayna?"

Interesting, Ryder thought when he saw a look pass between the two women. He knew the waitress, Melissa, began working at Mac's just before Rayna arrived in Serenity Springs, and she was also new to town. Could it be possible that they knew each other? Of course it was, he thought, lowering his head to hide his expression. The FBI wouldn't send her on a mission like this alone. He, Creed, and Katy had just assumed they were the only ones around who knew what was going on, but that was naïve thinking on their part. It would have been a stupid move sending Rayna in with just the Caldwells for backup, and the assistant director of the Federal Bureau of Investigations did not get where he was today by making stupid moves.

After the waitress left, Ryder changed the subject, talking about his mare that was about to foal. And when Melissa delivered their lunch, he pretended not to notice when Rayna slipped the napkin from under her plate into her pocket. She was good, very good. If he wasn't watching closely, he never would have noticed.

"Why don't you come by one night this week and see the ranch?" he offered, after they finished their dessert. "Or you could come out on Saturday? I have to ride out and fix some fence on the south end of our property. I would love the company."

He watched the war waging clearly in her eyes, hoping things would go his way, but knowing they probably wouldn't. He was right. "I don't think so, Ryder. I'm really busy with things right now."

"What things?" he could not resist asking.

"Staying alive," she whispered, with a sad smile.

"Rayna…"

She stood, reaching out to place a hand on his arm when he would have followed. "I'll try and come to see you soon."

I won't count on it, he thought as he watched her leave. Shaking his head, he stood, taking out some money and leaving it on the table. He didn't have the bill yet, but a fifty would cover it, and give the young waitress a decent tip. He'd had enough fun for the day. He needed to get his ass into work and hope his brother didn't beat the shit out of him for real this time.

Chapter 15

"So," Creed grumbled, when Ryder sat down across from him fifteen minutes later, "are you ready to talk about what's really bothering you?"

Ryder shrugged, tilting his Stetson back on his head, a small smirk forming on his lips. "Maybe I just liked to see what it takes to get under your skin? It is kind of fun to see you riled up."

Creed leaned back in his seat, crossed his arms over his massive chest, and cocked an eyebrow. "I call bullshit." When Ryder refused to respond, Creed asked, "How was lunch?"

"The food was good, and the company even better," Ryder replied, as he began to tap his fingers on his leg, in tune to a rhythm only he could hear. It was a song from long ago, one he had almost forgotten, written for a girl with long dark hair, and pretty brown eyes. Being with Rayna had him remembering so many things from the past, some good, some bad. This one was definitely in the good category. It filled him with happiness and made him itch for his guitar.

"Where do you want me today?"

"Jace will be by to pick you up soon." Creed hesitated a moment, "Ryder, do you think you should be spending time with Rayna?"

Ryder glared at his brother. He didn't have to explain himself to anyone, and right now he wasn't in the mood to listen to a lecture. "I think I better get to work."

"Look, Ryder," Creed sighed, leaning forward to rest his forearms on his desk, "all I'm trying to say is that it may not be the best idea to hook up with her." His eyes clouding over, he muttered, "The woman seems to have a death wish. She's on a mission right now that could get her killed. It wouldn't be good to get tangled up in that mess. Chances are, it won't end well."

"It's our job to make sure nothing happens to Rayna. Maybe you should worry about that instead of how much time I'm spending with her." Ryder's jaw tightened as he fought for control. Somehow the woman had already managed to get under his skin, and the thought of her dead made him want to beat the hell out of something. Instead of pulling his brother over the desk, and finishing what they started earlier, Ryder stood and walked to the door. Looking back, he told Creed, "What I do on my own time is none of your business."

"It is my business, dammit."

Ryder shook his head, pointing a finger at Creed. "You are my brother, Creed, not my keeper."

"Your damn right I'm your brother," Creed exploded, rising from his chair so quickly that he knocked it over. "I'm trying to look out for you, Ryder. We are family. It's what we do!"

Ryder stared at his brother for a moment before swallowing hard and looking away. "Right now, all I need is your support. I'm drawn to her, Creed. I don't know what it is about Rayna, but I want to spend time with her. Get to know the person she has become. A part of me cared deeply for her when we were kids, and I'm finding out those feelings are resurfacing." He'd never told his brothers or Katy about that summer he spent with Macey. He had come so close to asking her out, but in the end, he shied away from it, afraid it would ruin his friendship with her sister.

"I thought it was Olivia you loved?"

Ryder met his brother's gaze, wondering how much of his past to share with him. "Before Olivia, there was Macey," he finally responded, before turning and leaving the office.

Chapter 16

He'd finally found her. It had taken his snitch in the FBI long enough, but he finally knew where Macey Fuller, the daughter of the son of a bitch who tried to put him away years ago, was. Nobody went up against Diego Cortez and lived to tell about it. Nobody. He remembered the promise he made Robert Fuller years ago when he left the courtroom. It was a promise Diego intended to keep. The traitor's entire family would die.

Looking down at the file in front of him, a slow, evil grin spread across Diego's face as he picked up the picture on top. Dark brown hair, wide, captivating eyes, stunning in every way. Too bad he wouldn't be able to enjoy her for awhile before her death.

"Macey Fuller," he muttered in satisfaction, "you've broken your cover and moved back to Serenity Springs. You should not have let your emotions get in the way. Because you did, I now know not only who you are, but where to find you." Running his thumb down the side of the picture, he rasped, "You will die, just as I promised, but first...let's have a little fun."

Placing the picture back in the file, Diego shut it slowly. Picking up the phone, he made a call, giving the person on the other line specific details of the job he wanted done. "No, there is no rush with this one," he said quietly, "take your time. Play with her some first. Find out if there is anyone she is getting close to. I will use them as leverage and kill them if I have to. For now though, Macey is your main objective. Do not kill her before I give you the order. I will let you know when I am ready for it to be done."

Hanging up the phone, Diego leaned back in his chair, signaling to the woman who stood stiffly in the corner. "You have done good, my dear. You will be properly rewarded."

He fought the urge to laugh at the revulsion in the eyes staring back at him. He knew she didn't want to work for him. She had no choice. When he threatened someone, he threatened their entire family, and she loved hers very much.

Chapter 17

Rayna stood with her hands on her hips, a proud, satisfied smile on her lips, as she slowly gazed around the sparkling kitchen. She had never enjoyed cleaning, but it was one of those necessary evils. As hard as her mother tried to instill the importance of it in her, Rayna always slipped out in the middle of it every Saturday, and ended up helping her father outside.

Glancing at the clock, she realized it was early afternoon, and decided to head into town for a late lunch. Leaving the kitchen, Rayna paused at the sound of a vehicle coming down the road. Walking to the window, she peeked through the curtains and watched as a dark blue sedan turned and slowly made its way down the long driveway.

Rayna's eyes narrowed as she drew her gun. She did not recognize the car, and even though she highly doubted Cortez's men would show up at her door in broad daylight, it was better to be safe than dead.

As Rayna watched, the car stopped in front of the house. The door opened, and an older woman, tall and slim with dark hair speckled with grey, got out. After a quick look around, she leaned back into the vehicle and retrieved a large wicker basket. Slamming the door shut, she made her way across the lawn and up the steps to the front porch.

Rayna's heart dropped in her chest when she realized who the woman was. *No,* she thought, *why was she here?* Squeezing her eyes shut tightly, Rayna inhaled deeply, then slowly let the breath back out. After two more deep breaths, trying to calm her emotions, she placed her gun back in its holster. She would terrify the woman if she opened the door with her 9mm held high. After the second knock, she made herself holler out, "Coming!" as she went to the front door and unlocked it. Opening it, she tried to smile as she gazed into the beautiful green eyes of the Caldwell matriarch. Wondering briefly if her children had told her who Rayna was, she said politely, "Good afternoon, ma'am. What can I do for you?"

Holding out a hand, Cara replied, "I'm sorry it has taken me so long to make my way over here. I'm Cara Caldwell. My husband, two boys, and I live just over the hill. I wanted to welcome you to Serenity Springs." She handed the basket she held to Rayna. "I made some blueberry muffins for you, and there are a couple of apple cinnamon ones in there too." Laughing, Cara told her, "Caiden stole most of them this morning before I could stop him. They are his favorite."

Rayna accepted the basket, looking at it in surprise. The delicious smell coming from inside made her stomach grumble in hunger. “Please,” she finally said, “come in for a moment.”

Cara smiled, stepping into the house. “Thank you. I can’t stay too long. I promised my granddaughter I would take her riding after school today, but before that I have a couple of things that I need to do in town.” Looking past her, Cara said, “This house has always been one of my favorites around here. So large and inviting. I was happy to see the last owners kept it up the way that it should be.”

Rayna motioned towards the kitchen, still in shock that Cara Caldwell was standing in her foyer. “I’ve always loved it here,” she absently replied, and could have kicked herself the moment the words left her mouth. Ryder, Creed, and Katy were already a part of the clusterfuck she was in. There was no way she was going to allow their mother to be brought into it as well. She should not have even let her in the house. What the hell was she thinking? “Cara…”

Cara turned to look at her, understanding in her gaze, “Rayna, it’s okay. Let’s just go sit in the kitchen and eat one of these muffins. It has been a long time since I last saw you. Please, just give me fifteen minutes, and then I will go.”

Rayna’s eyes widened in surprise, and she took a hesitant step towards her. “You know who I am?” she asked. “Did Ryder tell you?”

"I've known who you were since the moment I saw you in town three weeks ago, child. I didn't need anyone to tell me."

"You can't be here, Cara," Rayna whispered, "It isn't safe. If something were to happen to you, I would never forgive myself."

Cara walked over, and gently cupped Rayna's chin in her hand. "Unfortunately, that is not your decision. I have lived a long, happy, and fulfilling life. God will take me when he is ready. It won't matter if I'm here with you, in town, or back home. It's not up to anyone but Him." Tugging Rayna close, Cara enveloped her in her arms and held her tightly. "I'm so glad you've come home, sweet Rayna. And I am so sorry that you are here alone this time. Maybe someday, you will tell me your story?"

She could not hold it in any longer. Rayna's body shook as she began to sob. She missed her parents so much. Her mother used to insist on giving all three of them a hug every night before bed, even when they were teenagers. Age did not matter, her mom always said, love did. "Someday," she promised, "if I make it through this."

Cara leaned back, smiling gently, "I have no doubt that you will, Macey Fuller, because no matter what you may think, you are not alone."

"Rayna," she choked out, "my name is Rayna now. Rayna Williams."

"Rayna," Cara said, patting her shoulder lightly, "I like it. It's strong, like you." Stepping back, she took the basket that Rayna clasped tightly in one hand from her, "Now, let's eat."

Rayna laughed softly, wiping the tears from her eyes, before following the other woman into her kitchen. As they chatted over muffins and coffee, all she could think about was that she had made a terrible mistake coming back to Serenity Springs. She was drawing a madman to this small town, to a family who accepted her for who she was, no matter if it was Macey Fuller or Rayna Williams. For the first time since she began working in law enforcement, Rayna began to rethink her plan to bring Diego down. Maybe what she and the FBI were planning was wrong. Maybe there was another way. There had to be. Because as much as she wanted to get Diego Cortez, it would kill her if she destroyed the Caldwell's lives in the process.

By the time Cara stood to leave, Rayna's mind was made up. She was going to call a meeting with the agents in town and tell them she had changed her mind. They would have to find another way to get to the mob boss. She was leaving Serenity Springs, and they were coming with her.

Chapter 18

Ryder talked softly to the dark brown mare that lay on the bed of hay, her breathing labored as she struggled to birth the foal who was coming too soon. Speaking gently to her, he watched as her eyes rolled up inside the lids, and a loud squeal of pain left her mouth. He ran a gentle hand down her neck and over her belly, wishing there was more he could do for her. Caiden would be there soon, and then he would take over. Something was wrong, and Ryder was afraid the foal was breach. He knew the steps to take if it was, but felt more comfortable with Caiden handling it. "Hold on, gal," he crooned, "help is on the way."

"What's wrong with her?"

Rayna's voice hit him hard, and Ryder fought the urge to turn and look at her. Keeping his concentration on the mare, he replied, "I think the foal is breach. Not only that, but it's early. Caiden will be here soon to take care of her."

"Is there anything I can do to help?" she asked. He heard her moving closer, and then she was there, kneeling beside him and reaching out to stroke the mare's nose. "What's her name?"

"Blue Moon," Ryder said, as he ran a hand over her back, "but we call her Blue."

"Because of her beautiful eyes."

"Yeah," he said shortly. Blue's eyes were a bright sapphire color, and although blue eyes were not necessarily uncommon for horses, they were unusual for a horse of her dark coloring. He was hoping the foal had them too.

"Hush, baby girl," Rayna whispered, stroking a hand down Blue's nose again. "Hush. I know you are in pain, but it won't be for much longer."

Ryder watched her out of the corner of his eye, wanting nothing more than to slip the lone strand of hair that had escaped from her ponytail back behind her ear. Remembering how soft it was made his fingers itch to touch it again, and he had to bite back a groan when his gaze traveled down the silky skin of her cheek to her full lips. Lips he desperately wanted to taste again, but with his tongue this time.

"Sorry it took so long for me to get here." His brother's voice interrupted his thoughts, and brought his mind back to the mare writhing in pain in front of him.

"She's not doing very well," he said, making himself move away from Blue so Caiden could get closer. "I have a feeling you are going to have to turn the foal."

Five minutes later, Caiden was agreeing with him. "I'm going to need you and…" his brow furrowed when he looked at Rayna. "Do I know you?"

"Her name's Rayna," Ryder said gruffly.

"Rayna," Caiden replied absently, his attention already back on the mare. "Hold Blue's head down, and both of you do what you can to keep her calm."

Ryder leaned over Blue's belly, stroking a hand down her chest as he talked softly into her ear, while Rayna continued to run a hand over her nose and neck.

Caiden swore roughly, and Ryder grunted when Blue moved quickly, striking him in the leg with one of her hooves. "Almost there," Caiden rasped, swearing softly again, but saying, "There we go. Now, how about we have a baby?" It wasn't long before a beautiful black and white foal lay next to her mother.

"What do you think?" Ryder asked Rayna after Blue and her baby were cleaned up, and the foal was nursing. "Ever seen anything like it?"

Rayna shook her head slowly, her eyes never leaving the foal. "No," she whispered, "never."

He chuckled softly as he watched his brother finish up with the mare. Now that the birthing was over, and everything was fine, he was exhausted.

"Now, she just needs a name," Caiden said, shutting the stall door behind him.

Rayna rested her hands on top of the door, her chin on her hands as she watched the little filly. "Heaven."

"What?"

"Her name should be Heaven, as in A Breath of Heaven, like the song. That's what she reminds me of."

"What song?" Caiden asked, "I don't think I've heard that one."

Ryder saw Rayna stiffen, before turning around to look at him. "It's just a song I know."

"It's a song I wrote when I was seventeen," Ryder told his brother, "but that's a story for another day. It's late, and I need some sleep, but first I want to talk to Rayna."

Caiden looked back and forth between Ryder and Rayna, before shaking his head. "I'll see you in the morning."

After he left, Ryder walked over to the front doors of the barn that were wide open, and looked up into the dark sky. "After I found out about the accident, I spent a lot of time outside at night, watching the stars, wondering if you were all up there looking down on us." Turning back, his heart skipped a beat at the sight of her leaning against one of the stalls, her arms crossed in front of her, and one leg raised, the heel of her boot against the wood behind her. Leaving the open doorway, he closed the distance between them, until he was so close they were almost touching. "I was so lost at first, Rayna. So upset, and angry at the world. I cared about all of you so much, you were a huge part of my life, and then you were just gone."

"Olivia was gone." Rayna murmured, "and you loved her."

Ryder moved closer, until their bodies touched, and he grasped the top of the stall door. "Yes," he admitted, "she was my best friend." Rayna ducked her chin, lowering her gaze from his. Ryder traced her cheek lightly with a finger, before cupping it gently in the palm of his hand and raising her eyes back to his. "Your sister is gone, Rayna, and as much as that hurts, we are both still here. We can't let the memory of her stand in the way of something that could be wonderful between us."

"There is more than just Olivia's memory standing in our way, Ryder," Rayna protested.

"Only if you let it." Ryder was tired of talking. *Fuck it,* he thought, leaning down to capture her mouth with his. He wanted to touch her, to feel her skin against his, to forget about everything except the way it felt when he was near her.

Ryder lightly traced her lips with his tongue, prodding gently, coaxing them apart. At first she was resistant, but then Rayna's mouth opened on a soft moan, welcoming him inside. He took swift advantage, slipping his tongue past her teeth, finding and tangling it with hers. She tasted so damn good.

Rayna's leg dropped from the wall behind her, and she pressed into him, clasping her hands tightly to his hips. A shudder ran through him when he felt her hand slide under his shirt and up his back. Her touch drove him wild, and he pushed his hard, aching cock into her stomach, hoping to relieve some of the pressure building up inside. Tearing his mouth from hers, he groaned her name, burying his face in her neck. "I want you, Rayna," he growled. "I need to be inside of you."

Rayna stiffened, and her hand stilled on his back. "I can't," she finally whispered. "I'm sorry, Ryder, I just can't right now."

Right now. She said not right now, but she didn't say that it would never happen. Her dark eyes were wide, deep swirls of brown full of unmasked desire, and he could feel her body trembling against his. Nodding, he muttered, "Then you better leave." When she hesitated, he chuckled, "I am agreeing to let you go tonight, even though I know you want me just as much as I want you, because not only do I respect your decision, but I don't want to take you in the barn that is close to where my parents are sleeping. But, baby, if you don't get the hell out of here, all bets are off."

Stepping back, Ryder allowed her to skirt around him and move quickly towards the door, but just before she reached it, he said, "Come to The Cavern Friday night."

Her hand resting on the barn door, Rayna turned back to look at him. "Why?"

He grinned, “Because I’m singing with one of the local bands, and I want to see you.” When she didn’t reply, he coaxed, “Come on, don’t make me beg.”

Rayna laughed, “Like you have ever had to beg for anything in your life, Caldwell.”

“I would if I knew it would get you there.”

Shaking her head, Rayna bit her bottom lip before saying, “Maybe.” She was gone before Ryder could respond.

Chapter 19

Rayna walked into The Cavern five nights later wondering what in the hell she was doing there. When she went to the Caldwell Ranch on Sunday, it was supposed to be to say goodbye. She had managed to get word to Lyssa that she wanted to have a meeting with her and Nathan as soon as possible. She was just waiting to hear back on a time and place. From what Rayna was able to find out, Nate normally came into town on Friday and Saturday, so she was hoping to have an answer soon. Until then, she needed to continue the charade, just in case anything changed.

The Cavern was a bar and grill opened five years ago by a couple of friends, Dale and Jack, who moved to Serenity Springs from Seattle, Washington. Originally, it was supposed to be just a bar, but two years into their venture, Dale jumped ship and returned to the city, leaving Jack full rights to everything. Jack was fond of good food, so he decided to add the grill, and now business was thriving. All of which Rayna heard about through the town grapevine.

Standing just inside the door, she allowed her eyes to adjust to the dim interior, as she scanned the building looking for Ryder. The band was not on stage yet, but there was a slow song playing, and several couples swayed back and forth in each other's arms. Once again, she wondered what the hell she was doing there when she spotted the entire Caldwell family sitting at a long table on the other side of the dance floor. Just as she was about to turn and run, she felt an arm slide around her waist. "Glad you could make it," a deep voice said near her ear, causing a shiver to run down her spine. Ryder. She was not in the room five minutes, and the man had already found her. So much for sneaking out.

"I came for the food and the music." And to see him maybe one last time, but he didn't need to know that. She almost did not come, but it had been so long since she heard him sing. The last time was several years ago when she found out he was playing at a small bar just outside of Dallas. She was unable to fight the urge to see him, and had gone, making sure to hide in the back. Unfortunately, it did not last long, because he almost caught her there. She'd left before he could recognize her, all the time wishing life had turned out so much differently.

"Sure you did," Ryder responded with a grin, guiding her toward his family's table. "Katy saved you a seat."

"Oh, she didn't have to do that. I just planned on sitting at the bar."

"Good luck with that. My mother admitted that she knows who you are, and we had to tell her what was going on. We were trying to keep everything far away from her, but you know my mother. She isn't going to let you out of her sight tonight." His blue eyes twinkled down at hers when he said, "She has decided that you are either moving in with us where we can keep you safe, or one of us is staying with you. Being the gentleman that I am, I volunteered to do the moving. Except, I refuse to sleep on that little couch of yours again. Good thing the bed is big enough for both of us."

Rayna's eyes narrowed, and she growled, "You better be kidding me, Ryder Caldwell."

Throwing his head back, Ryder laughed loudly, causing several people to turn and look at them. Rayna just shook her head, finally accepting defeat…for now. Sighing, she asked, "Does everyone in your family know who I am?"

"Yes," Ryder replied, "but I don't understand why that's a problem? You want to get Cortez here. He needs to know who you really are for that to happen."

Rayna stopped and turned to look up at him. "Yes, Ryder, I did want that, but not at the expense of your family."

Ryder pulled her out on the dance floor, tucking her close. "What do you mean when you say that you *did* want that?" he asked, his head bent to her ear.

Against her better judgment, Rayna snuggled deeper into his embrace, resting her head on his shoulder, and sliding an arm around his waist. It was so hard to fight her feelings for this man. "I've decided to leave Serenity Springs," she finally whispered.

She felt Ryder stiffen, his hand tightening on hers, "What do you mean? Why would you leave?"

"To keep you and your family safe," Rayna replied honestly.

"What about your safety?"

Rayna gently ran her hand down his chest, and then around his waist, holding him in a tight hug. "I haven't been safe since I was a child, Ryder."

"So you are just going to give up?"

Rayna shook her head slightly, "No, I'm not giving up. Just changing the playing field."

Ryder was silent for a moment before responding, "When you arrived, you said luring Cortez to Serenity Springs, getting him away from his home turf, would be the best way to take him down. I am assuming that the FBI agrees since they are backing the mission?"

Not sure where he was going with this, Rayna leaned back and looked up at him. "Yes, that's true. If I can get Diego here, away from all he knows, all of his hiding places and contacts in D.C., I think we have a chance of bringing him in. If he comes after me, tries to kill me, I will be able to put the bastard away for good this time. No one attempts to murder an FBI agent and sees the light of day again."

"Then you need to move forward with your plan, Rayna," Ryder insisted. "You need to take him down so that you can stop living your life in fear. So you can sleep at night, and allow yourself to have friends. So you can give this thing with us a chance."

"Ryder…"

"Look, maybe I'm being selfish, but dammit, Rayna, I care about you. I want you here, alive, and not scared out of your damn mind every time you close those beautiful eyes at night."

Why couldn't he understand? His entire family was at risk. She could not allow that. "I'm putting your whole family in danger, Ryder. The minute Diego Cortez finds out how I feel about you, about all of you, you will become a target."

Ryder lowered his head so their cheeks were touching, "Why don't you let us worry about that."

"Did you not hear what I said? He will send someone after you, Ryder. He will kill you, all of you, just like he did my family."

Ryder chuckled, nuzzling her cheek with his and placing a soft kiss at her temple. "If you think the Caldwells will bow down to a man like that, then you don't know us very well. We protect our family at all costs, Rayna, as well as those we care about."

She heard the underlying threat in his voice, and the claim in his words. He was telling her that he cared for her, and would protect her. For the first time in a long time, Rayna allowed herself to wonder what it would feel like to be loved by a man like Ryder Caldwell. He was the type of man who lived for his family, and would die for them if he had to. Lord help her, but she wanted a man like that in her life. Not just any man. She wanted Ryder.

Ryder stepped back from her as the song came to an end, catching her hand and threading his fingers with hers. They walked over to the table where the Caldwell family sat, his hand never leaving hers. Just when they reached it, someone began to announce the band that was playing that night. "I have to go play for a bit," Ryder said, smiling down at her, "but you are *not* leaving. When I'm done, we will figure out a way to fix the situation, instead of running from it." The last was said quietly, but with purpose. Raising their hands to his lips, he gently kissed the back of hers, before dropping it and walking to the stage.

Rayna watched him go, her emotions waging a war inside of her. She wanted to stay, but if she stayed, she could get them all killed. Ryder turned and looked at her, one foot on the step leading up to the side of the stage. Their eyes locked, and a slow, crooked grin crossed his mouth, making her heart skip a beat. Could she really leave this man without knowing what the future held? There was a time when she would have done anything to be with him.

"Have a seat, Rayna." Katy's voice broke through her thoughts, bringing her back to the present. "If you stare at my brother like that much longer, his ego will get much bigger than it already is, and none of us want that."

Her cheeks a fiery red, Rayna walked around to the other side of the table, dropping down into a chair in between Katy and Sloane. She noticed both Katy and Creed sat with their backs to the wall, where they could keep an eye on what was happening in the bar, and no one could sneak up on them. It was a habit of most police officers, and one Rayna followed herself. "Thanks," she said, her attention going back to the stage when the band started to play.

They were good, very good, and Rayna found it hard to tear her gaze away from Ryder to scan the room periodically for danger. Every so often, she would respond to a question asked by someone in his family, but for the most part, her eyes never left Ryder. Several questions played tug-a-war in her mind, the main one being, should she stay or should she go.

She was so enthralled with Ryder and his voice, that it took Rayna longer than normal to feel the eyes on her, watching her from across the room. A prickly feeling started at the base of her skull, slowly spreading out, and she froze, smiling at something Katy said as she began to scan the room. She relaxed somewhat when she found Nathan leaning against a wall talking to a pretty redhead. He looked over at her before glancing toward the bathrooms, then back at her. He wanted to talk.

Rising, Rayna told Katy that she would be right back. Making her way around the dance floor, she glanced at Ryder one last time before turning down the long hall that led to the restrooms. A small squeak left her when a hand clasped around her upper arm and she was yanked into a dark room, and the door shut quickly behind her. The punch she automatically threw out was blocked, and two arms wrapped around her tightly, holding her arms to her sides. "Stop it, Rayna," a gruff voice ordered, "it's just me."

"Nathan, what the hell? I could have hurt you!"

"You weren't doing a very good job of it yet," Nate scoffed, letting her go and stepping back.

Choosing to ignore the small jab, Rayna glared at him in the darkness. "What are we doing in here?"

"I was told you wanted a meeting, and we can't do that out there in front of a hundred people. Not without blowing my cover."

Rayna shoved her hands in her back pockets, indecision beating at her. "I was thinking about calling this whole thing off," she finally admitted. "I'm placing people I care about in danger. It just isn't sitting well with me."

"Well, you should have thought about that before we set the plan in motion," Nathan said, his voice low and rough. "It's too late now."

"What do you mean?"

"I mean, Diego took the bait. My sources tell me that he not only knows who you are, but he also knows that you are here, in Serenity Springs." She felt Nathan move past her, then a small sliver of light appeared when he cracked the door to the room open slightly. "You aren't going anywhere, sweetheart. Not until we catch this son of a bitch."

He was gone before she could respond. Following him into the empty hallway, Rayna used the restroom quickly before going back to the table. She looked at the family who meant so much to Ryder, horror filling her at what she was subjecting them to. What had she done?

"This next song is one I wrote when I was just a teenager." Still standing rooted to the spot by the table, Rayna turned to look at Ryder. "I wrote it for someone very special to me."

Ryder's eyes met hers, as his fingers began to slowly strum the guitar strings. Her heart clenched when his voice rang out over the room, strong and clear, singing a song from so long ago.

Eyes the color of the sweetest chocolate,

Light brown hair as soft as midnight rain,

A smile to match the clouds above,

A touch of her lips, is like a taste of heaven.

"I haven't heard him sing this song since before the accident," Cara said, her voice full of shock. Reaching over, she took hold of Rayna's hand. "I assumed it was about Olivia, and it hurt him too much to think about it."

Rayna's dark brown eyes sparkled with unshed tears, as she glanced over at Ryder's family. "I was there when Ryder wrote the song," she told them, "but it isn't about Olivia." Biting her lip to try and hold back the tears, she looked back at Ryder. His head was now bowed, his voice low as he sang. Slipping her fingers from Cara, she wiped at some tears that slipped free. "My sister had green eyes, like my mother's."

"Oh," she heard Sloane gasp loudly, "it was your song."

Rayna smiled at her through her tears. "Yes." Knowing she had to get out of there, Rayna told them goodbye quickly. After one last look at the man on stage who had captured her heart once before, and was on his way to wrangling it once again, she turned and ran.

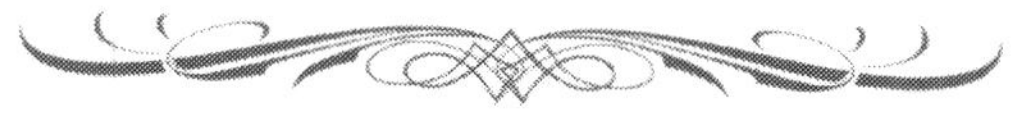

Ryder finished the last set, spoke with the band, and packed up his guitar, before making his way down to where his family waited. He'd seen Rayna leave earlier, and even though it bothered him that she walked out in the middle of their song, he understood. It had hit him just as hard singing it, as he was sure it hit her hearing it.

When he reached his family, he handed his guitar to Caiden. "Can you take this back home for me? I have somewhere I need to be."

"Son," his mom said, placing a hand on his arm, "try and go slow with Rayna. She is going through so much right now. I don't think you understand."

"I do, Mom" he said quietly, covering her hand with his.

"No," Cara shook her head, squeezing his arm gently, "I'm not talking about the reason she's here, son. I'm talking about her feelings for you."

Ryder leaned down and placed a soft kiss on his mom's cheek. "If it's anything like what I'm feeling for her, then we should be just fine."

"I hope so, but I get the feeling that she thinks she will always be living in her sister's shadow around you, Ryder. You need to show her that what she fears, just isn't true. I see the way you look at

Rayna, and it has absolutely nothing to do with Olivia."

Ryder hugged his mom close, thanking her, before saying goodbye to everyone and leaving The Cavern. His mother was wise beyond her years, and if she thought that was how Rayna felt, then he was sure it was true. Now he just needed to figure out how to change it.

Lost in his own thoughts, Ryder did not see the man watching him from the bar. The dark eyes were trained not only on Ryder, but on all of the people with him, and they gleamed with satisfaction.

Chapter 20

Rayna turned off the road, driving slowly down her driveway towards the house. When she left the bar earlier, she was too upset to come home. She needed time to think, so she took the highway south out of town and drove for almost fifty miles, her thoughts filled with Ryder and memories of her family. Two hours later, she had finally come to the conclusion that she was tired of living in the past. No one knew what the future held, but the present was here and now. And right now, what she wanted was to be with Ryder. She had no idea where it would lead, but she felt like she deserved the chance to find out. She could not change what was happening right now with Cortez. It would happen whether she was with Ryder or not. All she could do was do everything in her power to protect the people she cared about from whatever Diego sent their way.

Getting out of her car in front of the barn, Rayna ran and slid the large barn doors open, flipping on the lights. There was a storm coming, and she wanted her car out of it in case it hailed. She just barely got her vehicle inside the barn before the rain started. It beat down heavily on the old tin roof, and angry winds rattled the front doors. Rayna closed them most of the way, but kept them slightly ajar so that she could watch the storm. Several minutes later, she climbed the stairs on the side of the barn to the hayloft, and stood gazing around at the bales of hay that filled up half of the loft. The large floor was also covered in it, and one of the loft doors was open.

The people Rayna bought the farm from had horses, and when they moved, they left the hay because they did not want to transport it all of the way to Denver from Texas. The loft looked just like it did when she was a child. She remembered playing hide-and-seek with Matty in the barn. Laughing loudly, chasing each other around the loft, jumping over bales of hay. Where was that laughter when she needed it now? Where was that joy, the love from her family?

Rayna stiffened when she heard the distinct sound of the barn doors below opening, and then slamming shut. Was it Diego's men? She knew he would be coming for her. She had no idea how long it would take, but now that he had found her, he would be coming.

She heard footsteps on the stairs heading up to the loft. They were coming towards her. Removing her 9mm from its holster, she raised it, leveling it at the top of the stairs, before quickly lowering it again when Ryder's face came into view. His gaze on her, he crossed the floor, stopping in front of her.

Thunder rumbled across the sky, and lightening flashed as they stared at each other. "You left," he accused her quietly, his hands clenched tightly into fists at his sides. "You left."

He was mad because she left the bar? She'd had to leave. She had to get out of there. He was singing their song. The memories had torn through her, ravaging her heart. Stiffening her spine, she placed her hands on her hips and asked, "Ryder, where exactly do you see this going?" Ryder took another step toward her, but kept silent. She wanted to move forward with him, but she had to make sure she was the one he really wanted first. She refused to be the one he settled for because her sister was gone. Taking a deep breath, Rayna said, "I am not Olivia, Ryder."

"I know you're not," he growled, as he slowly reached out and caressed her cheek. "Olivia is gone, Rayna. She's dead. I know that."

"And I could be soon."

Ryder's eyes flashed in anger. "Don't you ever say that again!" he ordered. Sliding his hands into her hair, he held her firmly as his lips collided with hers. Rayna moaned as he thrust his tongue past her lips, finding hers. His hands tightened in her hair, holding her in place when she would have pulled back.

Rayna brought her hands up, clutching tightly to his shirt, swamped with emotions. Heat was rising inside of her, the need to touch him almost unbearable. Stepping closer, she returned Ryder's kiss desperately. He felt so good against her.

Slowly unclenching her hands, she reached down and tugged his shirt from his jeans. What she was about to do might be wrong, but she needed this man, more than she needed anything else right now. Giving up after unbuttoning the two buttons at the bottom of his shirt, she grabbed hold of it and ripped it open, buttons flying across the loft. She had to touch him, had to feel his skin against hers.

"Rayna," he groaned against her lips, pressing his lower body against hers. "Fuck," he moaned at the feel of her full breasts against him.

Tearing her mouth from his, she licked and sucked her way down his neck, and then over his chest tracing one of his tattoos with her tongue. His hands still clenched tightly in her hair, he groaned her name again as he guided her lower, over his stomach, and lower still.

Quickly undoing his belt buckle, Rayna unbuttoned his jeans and slid the zipper down. She glanced up at him, theirs eyes meeting as she slid her hands inside the waistband of his jeans, pulling them down over his hips, his boxer briefs quickly following. Dragging her eyes from Ryder's dark blue, hungry gaze, she lowered them to watch his cock as it sprang free. Grasping it in one hand, she leaned forward and licked the tip, before slowly enclosing as much of the thickness into her mouth as she could.

Both of Ryder's hands were threaded through her hair in a firm grip, holding her still as he pulled back, and then pushed forward into her mouth. "That feels so fucking good, Rayna," he groaned, doing it again, and again.

Rayna opened wider, allowing more of him inside her. Sliding her hands up and around to cup his bare ass, she dug her nails into the hot flesh as she allowed him to control the pace. Soon, Ryder pulled back, slipping from her mouth. When she would have protested, Ryder shook his head. "No. We have played around long enough, Rayna. I need to be inside of you. I want to feel you surround me. I need more than just your mouth. I need all of you."

Slowly standing, Rayna nodded, taking his hand. "No," Ryder protested. "I want you here. Right here." Sliding his hands down her sides, he gently pulled up her dress, slipping it over her head. Sliding out of his jeans, he walked over to a bed of hay and laid the dress out on top of it, along with his shirt. Slipping the belt out of the loops in his jeans, he placed them on the hay too. Looking back at her, he held out a hand.

Her eyes never leaving his, Rayna went to kick off her boots. "Leave them on," he growled, "they are sexy as hell."

Her heart pounding, Rayna undid the front clasp of her bra. Flipping it off over her shoulders, she let it fall to the ground, soon followed by the lavender panties she wore. She looked over to where Ryder waited, his hand still held out to her. Making her way toward him, she let her gaze wander over his hard, muscular body. A body that was kept that way from days of hard work on his ranch. Slipping her hand into his, she reached out with her other hand, trailing it over his bare chest and then down his abs. She had never met a man more breathtaking to her, and she could not stop touching him. He let her play for a minute, before pulling her close, capturing her mouth with his. He slipped his tongue into her mouth, claiming her once again as he slowly lowered her to the clothes. "You are so beautiful, Rayna," he whispered, leaning back to look into her eyes, "so beautiful."

Cupping her breast in his large hand, Ryder leaned down and playfully nipped at her nipple before circling it with his tongue and sucking it into his mouth. Rayna cried out when he tugged on it with his teeth, and then sucked again. "Ryder, please," she gasped, clutching his shoulders, trying to pull him up her body, "I need you."

Ryder moved over her, bracing his arms on the floor beside her head. Their eyes met, and Rayna dug her nails into his skin, as she raised her hips to him. Sinking his fingers into her hair, he covered her mouth with his as he pushed deep inside of her. Rayna cried out, bucking her hips into his, again and again, trying to get him to move.

Tearing his mouth from hers, Ryder rasped, "Slow down, sweetheart. I want to take my time and enjoy this."

"I can't," she gasped, as he slowly pulled out, then pushed back in. "Ryder!"

She felt one of his hands move down her side, and then slip under her leg, lifting it slightly as he drew back and then pushed deep inside her again. "You feel so good," he groaned, lifting her leg higher, and pushing in deeper. "So fucking good."

Rayna couldn't stay still. Need was rising inside of her, and soon had her begging and pleading with him to move faster, harder. Tightening her hold on his ass, she pushed up, meeting him thrust for thrust. Pleasure swamped her, and soon she could not hold back the scream that left her throat as an orgasm ripped through her. Ryder quickly followed, groaning her name as he came.

Rayna gasped for breath, as Ryder slowly pulled out of her and lay down, holding her close. Trailing his hand down over her rib cage, then back up to cup her breast in the palm of his hand, he muttered, "I don't think I can move, baby."

Snuggling close, Rayna murmured, "Me neither." She wanted to close her eyes, and fall asleep. She was so tired, and she felt safe next to Ryder, even if she was out in the middle of a barn, with no locks on the doors. "I should go inside," she said sleepily.

"Don't you mean we should?"

Shaking her head groggily, Rayna said, "No, we can't. I might hurt you."

"Rayna," he lowered his head to kiss her gently on the lips, "do you trust me?"

"Of course." There was no hesitation in her response. She trusted the man with her life. There was no question about it.

"Then let me spend the night." Rayna started to protest, but Ryder gently laid a finger over her mouth. "You need sleep. You said yourself you never rest more than a couple of hours at a time. Trust me. Let me watch over you while you sleep."

Opening her eyes to look at him, Rayna fought with herself before finally nodding. "Okay," she agreed.

"Okay?"

"Yes," she laughed, "okay."

It didn't take them long to get their clothes on and get to the house. They cleared the rooms quickly, making sure they were alone and that all windows and doors were locked, and then they went upstairs to her room.

"There's something you need to know," Rayna said, slipping on a pair of shorts and a tight tank top that scooped low in the front, cupping her breasts just right. Ryder bit back a groan as he forced his gaze away from the tantalizing sight before him, raising his eyes up to hers when she spoke. "I talked to one of my contacts tonight. Diego knows who I am, Ryder. He will be coming for me."

Ryder drew down the comforter, waiting while she slid into bed, and covering her with it. "Then he will have to go through me."

Smiling shakily, Rayna whispered, "That's what I'm afraid of."

Ryder leaned over and kissed her gently. Taking the gun she placed on the end table, he opened the drawer and slipped it inside. "This way it will be near you, but you won't be able to grab it and aim for me in the middle of a nightmare," he explained. After one last kiss, he drew his own gun and walked over to the window. Lowering himself to the long bench in front of it, he put his back against the wall, and his legs out in front of him. Placing his gun on his lap, he glanced back to her, "Get some rest honey. I will protect you."

As Rayna's eyes drifted shut, a small smile appeared on her lips. For once, someone was taking care of her, and it felt wonderful.

Chapter 21

The sun was just barely coming up over the horizon the next morning when Ryder heard Rayna begin to stir. As far as he could tell, she'd slept soundly, with no signs of a nightmare plaguing her. He watched as she turned from her side to her back, reaching her arms above her head to stretch languidly. Fighting back a groan at the sight of her nipples pressing against the light blue shirt she wore, Ryder reached down to adjust his rapidly growing erection. He made himself stay where he was, even though what he really wanted to do was join her in that bed and wake her up himself. But, he wasn't some horny teenager just out to get laid. No, he cared about Rayna. He was beginning to more than just care about her, but that was something he would keep to himself right now. He did not want to scare her off when she was finally starting to open up to him.

Rayna turned on her side, pulling her pillow close and snuggling into the covers with a small, sleepy smile on her lips. She looked happy. Not only that, but she looked at peace. So sweet and innocent. So different from the hard, determined FBI agent she normally appeared to be.

Just when Ryder was about to rise and stretch out his own aching muscles, Rayna's eyes opened, and she stiffened visibly when she saw him. "Hey beautiful," he said softly, grinning at the slight blush that covered her cheeks. "Good morning."

A tentative, answering smile crossed her face, before she murmured, "Good morning, cowboy."

Damn, he really wanted to crawl into that bed with her…so.fucking.bad. Remembering the feel of her skin against his the night before, the way she moaned when she came, had him hardening even more.

"Have you been sitting there all night?" Rayna asked softly, as she sat up and tucked the comforter around her breasts so just a small amount of cleavage was peeking out.

What had she asked? "Not all night," he rasped, rising from the bench. After putting his gun back in its holster, he walked toward her, hiding a grin at the sight of her eyes glued to his dick. He didn't even bother trying to hide how aroused he was. "I made a few trips through the house, just to make sure we were still alone."

Her gaze met his, her dark eyes wide. "You really did stay awake all night to protect me?"

Placing one knee on the bed, Ryder leaned forward, gently grasping her chin in his hand. "When I tell you I'm going to do something, sweetheart, I do it."

"Thank you." The words were spoken so softly, he almost didn't hear them.

"Guess what?"

Her lower lip trembled slightly as she whispered, "What?"

"We got through the whole night without you trying to shoot me." Ryder laughed at her look of shock. Leaning down, he kissed her lightly on the lips. "Not once did you reach for your gun. You know what that means, don't you?"

Rayna shook her head, and Ryder placed a small kiss between her eyes, right where her brows were wrinkled in confusion. "What?"

"That means you trust me."

"Of course I do. I told you that last night."

Chuckling, Ryder placed a kiss on the tip of her cute, little nose. "It also means that I get to come back and stay again tonight."

"Ryder," she began.

Running a hand down her soft hair, Ryder gave her one last, gentle kiss on the lips. "I need to get back to the ranch. I have to check on cattle, and feed the horses. I have a few other things to do too, but why don't you come by later today? You can see Heaven, and we can take a ride. Maybe have a picnic?"

He watched her eyes mist over slightly. "You named the foal Heaven?"

Ryder ran a finger lightly down her cheek, "No, you named her Heaven." Ignoring the tears in her eyes, knowing she would not want him to bring attention to them, he pressed her, "So, how about that picnic today?"

He watched the indecision on her face, before she nodded slowly. "Okay. Around noon or a little after?"

"I'll be waiting." Ryder stood, making his way to the door.

"Ryder?"

Turning back, his heart clenched at the breathtaking sight she made in the middle of a bed that was much too big for just one person. "Yes?"

"Are you sure you don't want to stay a little longer?"

Allowing his eyes to roam over her, he slowly shook his head. "Baby, I want nothing more than to stay here and make love to you all morning."

"Then why don't you?"

Ryder groaned as her gaze moved slowly down his body, her skin flushing a pretty pink. "Because, Rayna, as much as I want to feel you against me, to hear you scream my name when you come, I want something else even more."

Rayna's eyes widened, her gaze flying back to meet his. "What?" she breathed.

"You." Not quite ready to explain to her exactly what he meant by that, Ryder turned and left, letting her jump to her own conclusions for now.

Chapter 22

Nathan rubbed a hand over his face, glad to finally be back to his cabin where he could get some rest. After spending the night in the hills above Rayna's farm, peering through a sniper rifle, and making sure she was as safe as she could be, he was exhausted. He was used to being up hours on end while undercover, because you never knew who you could trust. But after one of his personal contacts he had keeping an eye on things back in D.C. called him and told him that Cortez knew where Rayna was, he had spent the past two nights watching over her, and worked all day on top of it. He needed a break. Thank God he had the day off at New Hope Ranch today. Rayna would be on full alert since he passed on his information to her, and he'd seen that Caldwell had spent the night with her too.

After slipping into a pair of dark grey jogging pants, Nathan brushed his teeth and used the restroom. It was just after eight in the morning. With any luck, he would be able to sleep until late afternoon. Unfortunately, luck was against him. Just as he was getting ready to slip into bed, there was a knock on the door. It could only be one of two people. And since one was out of town visiting his son for the weekend, it had to be his sexy-as-sin boss,

Harper Daley. She had been one hell of a surprise when he'd shown up at New Hope Ranch. His file said she was forty-six years old, but the woman didn't look a day over thirty-five. She was gorgeous, with blonde hair, light blue eyes, and a figure he could not keep his eyes off of. He'd caught himself staring more than once, hoping she never saw. He did not know what it was about the woman, but damn, he liked her…a lot.

Shoving a hand through his messy hair, he went to open the door. There on the other side stood Harper, in a snug white tank top and a pair of jeans that hugged her curves just right. "Morning, boss lady," he said with a grin. "What can I do for you?"

Harper smiled, "I need your help when you have time. The damn water heater went out in the main house last night. I tried to fix it, but can't figure out what's wrong. I'd ask Henry, but he's gone this weekend."

Against his better judgment, he unlocked the screen door and opened it. "Come in while I put some jeans on."

Harper strode past him, stopping in front of the rumpled bed. "Busy night?" she asked, turning to face him. Placing a hand on one hip, she cocked her head to the side and raised an eyebrow.

His gaze went from the bed to the pissed off woman. Hell, he hadn't even made it to bed yet, but he could not tell her that. "You could say that."

"You know the rules, Nate," Harper snapped, her eyes flashing in anger, "no women are allowed on the ranch!"

"Now Harper," he drawled, loving the way her name rolled off his tongue, "I have never brought a woman here, and I never will. I promised you that the day I started, and I always keep my promises." He loved the fiery glint in her eyes, and her take-no-shit attitude. Harper Daley was one of the strongest people he had ever met. She lived for the kids on her ranch. She would do anything for them, and he highly respected her for that. He had also never been so attracted to a woman before. That part was becoming a problem.

Harper's gaze broke away from his, landing on his bare chest. A dark flush covered her cheek bones, and her gaze lowered more still. "Thank you," she said, her tongue slipping out to trace her lower lip.

Oh fuck, he thought, as he felt himself thicken and harden. He couldn't help it. He wanted more than just her eyes on his body, he wanted that tongue licking where her eyes were wandering.

When her gaze rested on where his jogging pants hung low on his hips, a soft gasp escaped as she saw his obvious arousal. Turning away quickly, she crossed the room to stand by the window facing the pastures in the back of her property. There were several cabins on the ranch. Four of which housed the children ages twelve to seventeen. His was set apart from theirs, and was just two rooms. One large one with a small kitchen area and a place with his bed and a television, and then there was a small bathroom.

Unable to stop himself, unsure where the hell all of his self-control had gone, Nathan followed her across the room. He stopped right behind her, their bodies barely touching. Harper jumped when he placed his hands on her hips, stepping closer. He watched her hand tighten on the windowsill, a shudder running through her.

"What, you didn't get off last night?" she snapped.

Nathan smiled when he heard her breath quicken. "I wasn't with anyone last night, Harper," he said softly.

"Don't lie," she muttered. "You may not have done anything here, but I know you didn't come home, Nate."

How the hell did she know that? He was good at covering his tracks. Really good. "And how would you know that?" he questioned, lowering his head next to hers. "Did you come looking for me, Harper?"

Harper leaned her head back on his shoulder, another shudder running through her body. "Maybe," she murmured.

"Maybe?" he echoed, chuckling softly, as he slid his hand up some to rest on her rib cage, just below her heaving breasts. "Did you, or did you not, come looking for me, Harper?" he growled, nipping at the silky skin between her neck and shoulder with his teeth. He had never been this close to his employer before. Never talked to her like this. And she'd definitely never given off any vibes at all that even hinted she was attracted to him before. He had no idea what was going on, but there was no way he was going to stop it.

"I came because of the water heater," she gasped. "I tried to light it, but it wouldn't work. I didn't want to call anyone late at night, and Henry's in Dallas."

Thank fuck for broken water heaters, he thought, scraping his teeth lightly up her neck. Harper moaned, tilting her head to the side. There were so many reasons this should not be happening, but right now, he could not think of a single one. He traced the shell of her ear with the tip of his tongue, before tugging on her earlobe, and sucking it in his mouth.

"Oh God," she moaned. "Nate!" Harper pushed back against him, rubbing against his erection, as she reached back and slid her fingers in his hair. Clutching it tightly, she held him to her, gasping, "Nate, we can't do this. We can't."

He knew they couldn't, knew they shouldn't, but he did not give a damn. Tugging her shirt from the waistband of her jeans, he slid his hands up and cupped her firm breasts in his hands, flicking the nipples with his thumbs.

“Nate, please,” Harper moaned, reaching behind to slip her hand inside his jogging pants and grasping his hard cock. Nathan groaned when she began to stroke him, thrusting into her hand. He felt like a fucking teenager when his orgasm began to build quickly. Refusing to come without her, he flicked the button open on her jeans, and slid down the zipper. Slipping his hand inside, he slipped two fingers inside her, and began rubbing her clit with his thumb.

Nathan sucked on her neck, as he began to thrust into Harper’s hand matching the rhythm of his fingers moving inside of her. “Oh, Nate. Nate!” she cried out. “That feels so good. It’s been so long!”

“Come for me,” he ordered roughly, biting down gently on her shoulder as he increased the pace of his thrusts. He was so close, but he needed her there with him. “Harper, now!” he ordered.

A muffled scream tore from her, and he felt her begin to pulse against his fingers. Unable to wait any longer, he erupted in her hand. Lifting his head slightly, he looked down at her, where she lay panting on his shoulder. Her eyes slowly opened, looking so sexy clouded with passion.

Nathan saw the moment the regret began to creep into her face. Before she could speak, he covered her lips with his. He needed to taste them just once, before she shut him out. Just this one time, he wanted to feel them against his. Holding her head in place, he gently stroked at her lips until she opened for him, and he slipped inside. It was even better than he had imagined. But, soon, she was pushing him away. “No, Nate. We should not have done this.”

He knew she was right. There were so many reasons on his end as to why this could go horribly wrong, but it felt so right at the time. Slowly, he removed his hands from her jeans, and adjusted his jogging pants.

“Nate, that can never happen again.”

What the hell was her problem? He knew why it would be wrong for him to give in to the need to have her again, but why was she so against it?

Falling into his Nate persona to hide his true emotions, he grinned, “Why not? It seemed to have worked out great for us both this time.” That was not even close to what he really wanted to say, but it was what Nate would say. “I would think the next time would be even better.”

“There isn’t going to be a next time,” Harper insisted. After adjusting her clothes, she looked at him, “First of all, you are so damn young. I’m pushing fifty.”

Nate laughed. If she only knew how old he really was. “Age is just a number.”

Shaking her head, Harper said, “I’m way too old for you.”

Nate grinned, “Honey, if that’s all you got, it’s definitely not enough.”

"It's more than that," Harper said. "This ranch means everything to me. New Hope Ranch, these kids, it's all I have. You are here now, but you will be moving on."

"I don't understand," he told her, even though it was a lie. He knew exactly what she meant. He spent all of his life avoiding relationships, for that very reason. He'd never been able to settle down in one place for too long. "I'm here now."

"That's just it," Harper said, slowly shaking her head. "I'm not the kind of woman who just hops into bed with a man. When I give myself to someone, there needs to be a relationship. I don't sleep around. I can't afford to. I can't have that kind of reputation. Not when I own a ranch like New Hope."

"What makes you think I will leave?" he asked curiously.

Harper smiled, a smile that didn't reach her eyes, "You have that look about you."

"What look?"

"The one that says you are looking for something, but you haven't found it yet. You will roam until you find it, if you ever do."

Nate watched Harper turn and leave the cabin, shutting the door quietly behind her. She was right. He had spent his whole life looking for something that was always just out of reach. And now, he was wondering if he'd finally found it. If he had, could he keep it once Harper found out about all of his lies and deceit?

Chapter 23

Rayna grabbed the large insulated cooler bag filled with cold fried chicken, watermelon, potato salad, and bottled water off her kitchen table, sliding the strap over her shoulder. It was just past noon, and she was in a hurry to get to the Caldwell Ranch. She knew Ryder wasn't expecting her to bring lunch, but she wanted to surprise him.

After locking the door, Rayna left the front porch, heading for the barn where her car was parked. Her thoughts on Ryder and Heaven, she almost missed the fact that her barn doors were slightly ajar. She knew they were shut tightly the night before when she and Ryder left the building. She'd double checked them herself. There would have been no reason for Ryder to visit the barn before he left this morning, so that only meant one thing. Diego's man was close.

Quickly scanning what she could of the barn in front of her, Rayna slipped her hand over the butt of her gun letting the cooler fall to the ground. Sliding the 9mm from its holster, she sprinted across the lawn, stopping to the left of one of the barn doors. Her back up against the wall, she slowly made her way over until she could just barely see through the small opening between the two doors. Pressing her ear against the wood, she listened carefully, before sliding the doors open just wide enough to allow her to slip inside. She had a feeling that she was not going to find anyone hiding in the barn, but she needed to be cautious just in case.

Slowly, Rayna made a full sweep of the area, before swiftly climbing the stairs to the loft above. All was quiet, nothing seemed out of place, but she knew someone had been there. She could feel it. One thing she learned throughout her years in law enforcement was to always trust her instincts, and right now they were screaming at her that her barn had a visitor the night before.

After checking over her car to make sure it wasn't tampered with, Rayna walked back to the barn doors, opening them wide. Retrieving the bag from the ground, she stalked back to the car and threw it in the passenger seat. Getting in, she slammed her door shut before hitting the steering wheel with the palm of her hand. The son of a bitch was fucking with her. He was playing her, seeing how far he could go without her finding out who and where he was. He started out small, just to see if she was paying attention, and she had no doubt that he had eyes on her right at that moment.

Putting the car into gear, Rayna left the barn, heading down the long driveway, and taking a right onto the gravel road in front of the farm. Instead of heading toward the Caldwell Ranch, she drove away from it. As much as she wanted to spend the day with Ryder, she refused to lead anyone right to his ranch. No matter what the Caldwell family might say, she was not going to intentionally put them in harm's way.

Ryder waited all day for Rayna to show up at the ranch. After working hard that morning to get his chores done before she arrived, he brought Cochise and a pretty Appaloosa mare in from the pasture, brushing them until their coats shined. He and Rayna were going to go on a long ride, stopping by a pond on the far end of the Caldwell property for lunch, and maybe a few stolen kisses. He had it all planned out, had everything ready to go, but she never showed up.

A part of him wondered if she had just blown him off, but another part said there was no way Rayna would do that to him. Not after the night they just spent together. Not only that, but she told him when he left that morning that she would be there. She would not go back on her word.

Ryder would have tried calling her, but somehow he neglected to get her number, something he intended to correct as soon as possible. He did call Creed and Katy, only to find out that they did not have Rayna's number either.

Finally, in the late afternoon, Ryder gave up trying to be patient, and went to her house. Her car was gone, and everything was quiet. He sat on the top step of Rayna's porch, leaning back against the railing, one knee raised, and his Stetson pulled down low over his eyes. At first he was worried that something was wrong, but the longer he waited, anger slowly began to build inside of him. He may not have her number, but he knew damn well she had all of theirs. Katy gave them to her after she first arrived in case she needed anything. Not only that, but the Caldwell Ranch had a landline, and was easy to track down. Sitting here, waiting to see if she was dead or alive, was bullshit. He knew he was acting like a lovesick fool, but a part of him was really afraid Diego had already gotten to her.

By the time Rayna's car turned into the drive, his anger was at a slow boil. When she got out of the car, retrieving several bags from the back seat, it took everything in him not to get up and just walk away. She was out shopping all day. He was worried sick about her, afraid Cortez's men had her somewhere doing God knew what to her, and she was out fucking shopping.

"Hi," Rayna said, stopping at the bottom of the stairs.

"Hey," he replied shortly. Rising, he nodded towards her bags, "I see you've been busy today."

He watched as her eyes strayed from him, slowly scanning the farm, before coming back to him again. "Yes, I decided to go to Dallas today. There were some things I needed." He could hear the lie in her voice, and it just pissed him off even more.

Ryder pushed his hat back on his head, his eyes darkening into stormy clouds, "Did you have a good time?"

Rayna let out a short laugh. "Not at all." Before Ryder could respond, she motioned toward the house, "Why don't you come inside for a few minutes? We can talk there." His eyes narrowed in suspicion. Something was off with her, but he could not figure out what. "Now," she ordered softly, barely moving her lips.

Holding out a hand, she smiled when Ryder took it. His eyes full of suspicion, he followed her to the door, waiting while she unlocked it. The moment they were in the house, he shut the door and grabbed her arm, swinging her around to look at him. "What's going on, Rayna?"

Rayna dropped the bags to her feet, putting a finger to her lips. Taking out her gun, she pointed to him, and then motioned downstairs. Then she pointed to herself and nodded upstairs. Removing his own gun, Ryder quickly moved across the floor, staying away from the windows. It did not take him long to clear the rooms in the lower level of the house. As soon as he was done, he made his way to the upper level, meeting Rayna at the top of the stairs. Shaking his head, he remained quiet.

"He hasn't been in here yet," Rayna murmured, putting her gun away. "He will make his move soon, though."

"Dammit, Rayna," Ryder growled, pulling her close. "Tell me what's going on."

Rayna shrugged, turning away. "I don't know if anything is," she said evasively.

"Rayna," he said roughly, reaching out to grasp her hand in his, turning her around to face him. "Talk to me. Tell me what's going on. Why the hell didn't you come to the ranch today?"

"I couldn't," was all she would say.

"You couldn't?"

"No, I couldn't. Look, Ryder, maybe it would be best if we don't do this."

"What the hell is that supposed to mean?" She was trying to push him away, but he could tell she didn't want to. It was there, in her eyes, all of her emotions for him to see. She was not very good at hiding her feelings.

"This," she said, "you and me. It's not going to work out. Who are we kidding?"

"And why exactly is that?" he asked.

Rayna let out a short, humorless laugh, tugging her hand from his. "Seriously, Ryder, do you really even need to ask?" Shaking her head, she gestured at herself, "Dead girl walking here."

Ryder yanked her into his arms, refusing to listen to her talk like she was already gone. She let out a soft cry, caught off guard, her arms going to his shoulders to steady herself. "Don't you *ever* say that again," he ordered, "and get that thought out of your head. You are not going to die."

Her eyes clouding with sadness, she whispered, "Unfortunately, that isn't up to you or me, Ryder."

"Wanna bet?" His lips connected roughly with hers as he pulled her tighter against him, swallowing her protests. He would not listen to her talk as if she were already dead. He lost her once, it wasn't going to happen again. The feel of her lips against his, had him hard within seconds. He wanted nothing more than to sink deep inside of her, to feel her heat surround him, like he had the night before. But he had a feeling if he rushed her, it would just push her away.

Slowly easing back, Ryder trailed his knuckles down the side of her face. "You are *not* going to die, sweetheart," he promised. "I won't let that happen." Leaning down, he gave her one last kiss before stepping back. "I have no idea why you didn't show up today. Maybe you did need to go shopping, maybe you felt threatened by what we shared last night. Hell, maybe you just plain didn't want to spend the day with me. I don't know. What I do know, is that I am not going to allow you to push me away,

Rayna Williams. I refuse to lose you again." As her eyes widened in surprise, he went on, "You do whatever you have to do, but I am not going anywhere."

"It's late, Ryder."

"Yes, it is," he agreed, "so I suggest we eat some dinner, watch a little T.V., and then go to bed."

"Bed?"

"Did you think I was kidding when I told you my Mama said one of us is to stay with you at night? I don't know about you, but I'm not going to tell her no." There was no way he was leaving her alone. He had no idea what was going on, but something wasn't right.

Chapter 24

Rayna stared in shock when Ryder turned and walked down the stairs. He was really staying. It wasn't safe for him to be here with her. After studying Diego closely over the years, she knew how he worked. He may just be messing with her right now, but he would order his man to kill Ryder just for the hell of it, just to see if it hurt her. And it would. It would break her heart.

She had seen the look in Ryder's face, the resolve and determination, he wasn't leaving. And to be honest, she didn't want him to. She was tired of being alone. Then there was what he said about not losing her again. What did he mean by that?

Rayna heard the front door open, then close. Walking into Matty's old room, she looked out the window, watching as Ryder cleared the front porch steps two at a time. Going to his truck, he retrieved a large duffle bag from the back. Well, if he wasn't going to leave, then she was going to have to go on the offensive. Instead of allowing herself to be hunted, she was going to have to become the hunter. And, somehow, she was going to have to keep the man she was falling for safe at the same time.

"Rayna?"

Realizing that not only was Ryder no longer outside, but he was back upstairs with her, Rayna turned to look at him. He stood in front of her room, bag in hand, eyeing her with concern. Closing the distance between them, Rayna leaned her head against his chest, loving how safe she suddenly felt. Ryder was here, with her, wanting to protect her. Even though he probably thought she blew him off earlier, he was still here now.

Leaning back, she looked up at him, wanting more than she would probably ever get from him. Slipping her fingers into his, Rayna walked into her bedroom and sat on the foot of her bed. "I'm so tired, Ryder," she admitted softly. "So damn tired."

Ryder sat beside her, turning his hand over to lightly trace her fingers with his. "Don't fight me on staying, Rayna. Let me keep you safe. You will be able to get the sleep you need."

Rayna rested her hand on top of his, squeezing it gently. "You need your rest too, Ryder."

"I get enough sleep," he said roughly. "Let me do this for you."

Rayna slowly shook her head, fighting back the tears that threatened to fall. "I don't just mean I'm tired physically." Her eyes meeting his, she whispered, "I'm tired of everything, Ryder. Everything. I'm tired of running, tired of constantly having to look over my shoulder, tired of putting on a brave front when all I want to do is crawl into a hole and hide. Tired of…" she paused, unsure if she should admit the rest.

"Tell me," Ryder ordered quietly.

A lone tear slipped free, trailing down her cheek as she whispered, "I'm tired of never allowing anyone to get close to me. Never letting myself feel anything, for anyone, because I'm afraid of what Diego will do if he finds out. Just once I want to let someone in. Just once, I want to care about someone, and have them feel the same for me."

"So, what's stopping you?" Ryder asked gruffly, reaching out to thread his fingers through her hair.

"The man who was in my barn at some point between the time we left it last night, and when I went to get my car to come see you for lunch, for starters." Shaking her head in dismay, she groused, "I even packed a lunch. Fried chicken, one of my favorites."

"Wait, you were on your way to see me? With lunch?"

"I wanted to spend the day with you," Rayna admitted, "but when I went to the barn, I saw that the doors were open a little ways."

"What happened?"

As much as Rayna wanted to keep Ryder far away from the bastard who was screwing with her, she knew it wasn't going to be possible, and he needed to be prepared. "Nothing, really. I cased out the entire barn, but nothing else was out of place."

"Then how do you know someone was here?"

"Let's just say that I heard from my contacts in the bureau, and Diego is on the move," she said evasively. She would not bring Nathan into the conversation. No one knew he worked with her, and that was the way she was going to keep it.

Ryder's hand tightened on hers. "He's coming this way?"

"I doubt he does right now. He will send someone else here first to try and take me out. When they don't succeed, he will either send more of his goons, or come himself. I don't know for sure."

"And you think that person is here already? That he has been in the barn?" Ryder's voice vibrated deeply with both anger and concern.

"I do. I know how the mob works, Ryder. He left those doors open for one reason, and one reason only."

When she didn't go on, Ryder asked, "And that is?"

"He's fucking with me. He wants to see if I'm on my game or not." Looking down at their clasped hands, she murmured, "I fell for it, and I made a mistake today, one I won't make again."

"What?"

"I went into that barn with my gun drawn, ready to take on the world."

"I don't understand the part where you did something wrong," Ryder said. "Sounds like you did the right thing to me."

"Exactly my point." Rayna leaned her head against Ryder's shoulder, closing her eyes. "The son of a bitch was probably watching me the whole time. Now he knows I'm onto him. It just became a game of cat and mouse, and I'm the mouse." At least that was what he thought. Rayna had never been a mouse, and she sure as hell was not going to start acting like one now.

"That makes sense," Ryder finally said, after thinking it over. "What do we do now?"

We don't do anything, Rayna thought, as she raised her head to look at him. A small smile covered her lips, and she said, "Now, we eat. Tell me, what's in that cooler you brought?"

It was obvious Ryder recognized that she was deliberately changing the subject by the darkening of his eyes, but he let her by with it. His lips turned up slightly at the corner, and he rose from the bed, pulling her up beside him. "Steak, and it's a damn good thing I packed that cooler with plenty of ice, or it would already be cooked."

Rayna grinned, "Nobody likes a smartass, Ryder Caldwell."

Chapter 25

Ryder left Rayna's house reluctantly early the next morning. As much as he wanted to be with her, he still had obligations at the ranch. Not only that, but it was Sunday, if he did not show up for church, he would have to deal with his mother's disapproval the rest of the day. Cara Caldwell attended service every Sunday, and unless her children were physically incapable of being there for some reason, they better be sitting in that pew beside her. He had invited Rayna to go with him, but was not surprised when she turned the invitation down.

Riding into town with Caiden, Ryder let his eyes drift shut for the brief time it took to get there. He was utterly exhausted after staying awake two nights in a row. He managed to get a two hour nap in the day before, but it was all catching up with him quickly. It seemed like he just closed his eyes, when Caiden was shaking him awake. "Come on, man. We're running late. You can get some sleep later."

Later? That was what he was always telling himself. Sleep was overrated. But, if he didn't get some soon, he wouldn't be able to protect his woman. His woman. Ryder felt a goofy smile form on his lips. He liked the sound of that. Rayna Williams was his.

"Ryder, seriously, get it in gear," Caiden muttered, opening his door. "Mom's going to kick our butts if we walk in there after the service starts."

Ryder slid from the truck and followed his brother into the church, praying he would be able to stay awake the full hour. His mom and dad both would kill him if he started snoring during the sermon. Soon he found himself sitting between Caiden and Katy, fighting to keep his eyes open. It was a battle, but they finally hit the closing prayer and he rose afterwards with his family to head home. He had to check on Heaven, feed the kittens in the loft, check on the cattle that he put in the north pasture the day before. The list went on and on.

"Ryder, what do you think?"

Katy's voice interrupted his thoughts, and he looked down at her earnest expression, unsure how to respond. He had no idea what she was asking him, and suddenly it seemed imperative that he find a seat, before he fell down. "Ryder? Are you okay?"

Ryder slowly shook his head, realizing they were now in the parking lot, close to Caiden's truck. "I need to sit down," he rasped, shaking his head to try and clear the fog from it. What was wrong with him?

Vaguely, he heard Katy calling for his brothers, then he felt an arm go around his waist as someone practically carried him to the vehicle. "Ryder." He recognized Creed's voice, but it seemed so far away. “Ryder, we are going to take you to the hospital. Stay with me, little brother.”

“No,” Ryder croaked, prying his eyes open as far as he could. Peeking through little slits, he grunted, “Rayna. Need Rayna.”

He heard a flurry of voices after that, but could not make out any of them. There was a ringing in his ears that grew louder and louder, and then it was over, as he slipped into oblivion.

Rayna was up with Ryder that morning, and as soon as he left, she canvased the entire barn again, along with her car and the house. She found what was left for her on the car, and after close consideration, she found something else in the kitchen and in the master bedroom. The asshole had been inside her fucking house, and she never knew. Going to her car, she collected the boxes in the trunk, more purchases from the day before that she forgot to tell Ryder about. After installing small cameras in every room in the house, Rayna hooked the system up to her phone so that she could watch all activity in the house on her phone. Things were about to get interesting.

After another quick look around the entire house, including the basement, Rayna took a quick shower and went downstairs to get some breakfast.

She was sitting at her kitchen table eating a bagel when there was a knock on her door. Picking up her gun from where it set on the table beside her, she moved slowly into the living room, looking out one of the windows, before quickly putting the gun away again. What the hell was Creed Caldwell doing at her door?

"Ryder needs you," were the first words out of his mouth when she opened the door.

"Is he at the ranch?"

"No, the hospital."

"Stop growling like a big ole bear, Creed," Sloane ordered, from where she waited in his truck. "You are going to scare the woman."

"Scare her?" Creed groused. "She carries a gun, Sloane. I highly doubt she is afraid of me."

"Why is Ryder at the hospital?" Rayna interjected, hearing only the fact that something was wrong with Ryder. "What happened?" Making sure she had her keys, Rayna left the house, shutting the door behind her. When she got to the bottom of the front porch steps, she looked behind her to find Creed still standing in the same spot he was in when she opened the door to him moments before. "What happened to Ryder?" She demanded, already afraid she knew the answer. He had stayed with her again, and it put him in danger.

"We don't know," Sloane told her, her voice carrying over the yard. "He lost consciousness at church this morning, so Caiden took him to the hospital. The rest of the family went with them, while Creed and I came to get you."

"Why?"

"Why what?" Sloane asked.

"Why did you come here?"

"Because my brother asked for you before he passed out," Creed said gruffly, finally moving towards her. "He says he needs you, so I'm taking you to him."

"But you don't want to," Rayna guessed, hearing the anger resonating deep in his voice. "You think this is happening because of me."

"Is it?"

"I have no idea," Rayna replied honestly, "but I hope not."

"Me too," Creed growled, stalking past her to get to his truck.

Ignoring his bad attitude, Rayna went to her own car. She knew where the hospital was. She didn't need an ass like Creed to show her how to get there. Raking a hand through her hair in frustration, Rayna grumbled to herself, "He may be an ass, but it's just because he loves his brother. I would be the same way."

Not bothering to wait for Creed and Sloane, Rayna put her car in gear and headed toward the hospital, missing the movement by the open hayloft door as she drove by.

She was good, but not as good as he had hoped. He'd all but waved to her from his hiding spot, and not once did she look up. Not only that, but she was obviously looking for something this morning, but it didn't look like she found any of the clues he left for her. All were exactly the same as when he left them, except for the barn doors. He knew for a fact that she saw those the day before. However, she missed what he left in the car, and he was sure that she did not even notice that he'd been in her house. He was tired of playing with someone that was below his standards. He was ready to finish the job and move onto something more worthy of his time.

Picking up his phone, he dialed his boss. "She's lacking in most ways," he said the minute the call was answered. "This is getting boring. Let me take her out now."

Once his request was approved, he hung the phone up with a small grin. Now things were about to get interesting.

Chapter 26

Ryder opened his eyes groggily, slowly turning his head as he tried to figure out where he was. There was an annoying beeping noise coming from one side of him, and soft conversation from the other. His head pounded, a dull, aching throb. What the hell happened? He remembered talking to his sister, and walking out of the church. That was it. There was nothing after that.

"So, you have finally come back to us, young man," a gentle, comforting voice said as a cool hand pressed against his forehead. "You had your family awfully worried there for awhile." Worried…there was something he should be worried about. What was it?

"Rayna!" her name left his lips on a shout as he rose up in bed, grunting at the pain that shot up the back of his neck and into his skull. "Where the fuck is Rayna?" he demanded, trying to remove the IV from his arm. The need to find her and make sure she was alright pushed at him, making him yank the covers aside and attempt to stand.

"She's fine, Ryder. Sit down."

Ryder fought against the strong hands that held him to the bed. He had to find her. Had to make sure she was okay. "Something's wrong with me,

Caiden. What if that bastard did something to me, and got to Rayna too? We need to find her."

"I'm right here, Ryder. I'm safe." Her voice soothed him, causing him to stiffen first, but then slump against his brother. He didn't fight anymore when he realized that she was there with him, and let Caiden help him back into the bed.

"Rayna," he rasped, holding out his hand. "Come here." He needed to feel her close. Needed her next to him.

"Hush," Rayna whispered softly, sitting on the bed beside him. He leaned into her touch when she gently moved a lock of hair back from his forehead. "I'm here with you now. You're going to be just fine."

"I'm not worried about me," he told her, clasping the hand she slipped into his tightly. "I thought something might have happened to you."

"I don't know what you all are talking about," a deep voice said from the doorway, "but this young lady looks just fine, Ryder Caldwell, and what's wrong with you can easily be fixed in a couple of days."

Opening his eyes, Ryder glanced at Dr. Winninghoff as he strode into the room. The man had been the Caldwell's primary physician since he and his siblings were children. He watched as the doctor greeted his parents, and then Caiden, Katy, and Creed. "Where's Sloane?"

"She took Cassie to get some lunch," Creed said, coming to stand beside the bed, on the other side from where Rayna sat. "My little girl is pretty upset. She's worried about you, Ryder. We all are." Creed's eyes hardened when they settled on Rayna. "Why don't you tell us what's going on, Doc? What's wrong with my brother?"

Ryder held tightly to Rayna's hand when she tried to pull back from him, glaring at Creed. "Watch yourself, Creed," he growled quietly.

"Boys, stop it. Now." Cara ordered. "I, for one, would like to know what is really wrong with my son. I have no doubt it is not Rayna. He hasn't been himself for months now. It started way before she came home."

"It's quite simple, actually," Dr. Winninghoff said, smiling kindly at all of them, "Ryder is just plain exhausted."

"So, it is her fault," Creed muttered, glaring at Rayna. "He's spent the last few nights over at her house watching over her while she slept. Protecting her and not taking care of himself."

"I am going to tell you one more time to shut your fucking mouth, Creed," Ryder said, his voice low.

"And then what?" Creed shot back.

"Then I'm going to get out of this bed and kick your…"

"Boys, that is *enough!*" Charles Caldwell's voice rang out loud and clear in the room, and there was immediate silence. Their father did not raise his voice often, but when he did, you listened. "Ryder has done nothing that you didn't do with Sloane, Creed. When she was threatened after moving here, not only did you sit outside her apartment at night to make sure she was safe, your brothers and sister did as well. Maybe you should think about that? Instead of condemning the woman he has come to care deeply for, maybe you should be stepping up to help him, the way he helped you. The way he helps everyone. That man works harder than anyone in this room. He is up at the crack of dawn, if not earlier, to get his chores done on the ranch before he comes to work for you. He doesn't have to help at the station, but he does because he knows you need him. He helps Caiden at the veterinarian practice if he needs to. Hell, he even helped the neighbor three weekends ago, then came home and worked all night on his own things in the barn."

"Dad…"

"No," Charles held up a hand when Ryder tried to interrupt, "no one else seems to see everything that you do, son, but your mother and I do. We know how hard you work, and we know what a good man you are. And even if your bullheaded brother can't see it, we know that Rayna is good for you. We've seen it in the way you act lately. You're happy, Ryder. Really happy. It's been a long time since we have seen you that way." Ryder watched in shock as tears filled his father's eyes. "You always have a smile on your face, always are the first one to step up and volunteer to help when asked, but your mother and I know you better than anyone. You were not truly happy until Rayna came home. Nothing you have done for her these past few days has put you in this hospital, son. It was everything you did for everyone else before that."

"It's true," Dr. Winninghoff agreed quietly. "You push yourself too hard, Ryder. All the sleepless nights over the past few months, working so hard to keep everyone happy, helping everyone out in need at the expense of yourself, *that* is how you ended up in here."

"Well, shit," Creed grunted, removing his Stetson and running a hand through his thick dark hair. "It would seem I owe you an apology, Rayna."

Rayna shook her head, "No, you don't. You were right. It may not be just my fault that Ryder ended up in the hospital, but I'm to blame too."

"No one is to blame," Cara said, coming forward to slide her arm around Rayna's shoulder. "Your father is right though," she continued, looking at her children in disapproval. "Ryder has been at Rayna's house the past couple of nights watching over her, and where have you been? He needed your help. Rayna's in trouble. He was there for Sloane."

“That’s different,” Creed started to say.

Cara cut him off, “Exactly how is that different? Sloane had a stalker, one who endangered all of our lives, along with the lives of every child in the Serenity Springs Elementary School. I don’t give a damn who is after this woman, Creed. Ryder cares for her. That makes her ours to protect.”

Katy’s eyes lowered in shame, and she agreed, “You’re right, Mama.”

“No one needs to protect me,” Rayna interjected. “I appreciate it, Mr. and Mrs. Caldwell, more than you will ever know, but I’m a federal agent. I can take care of myself.”

“Everyone needs help sometimes, child,” Cara said, hugging Rayna to her. “Accept it, because my children are going to give it whether you want it or not.” Her eyes turned to steel as she looked at first Creed, then Caiden, then Katy. “Who’s up first? It’s obvious Ryder won’t be able to be there tonight.”

Pride filled Ryder as he grinned at his mother. This was why he didn’t give a damn who his biological parents were. Charles and Cara were all he would ever need. “I will be there, mom. I’m going to stay with Rayna.”

“No, actually, you aren’t,” Rayna said, rising from the bed, and leaning over to give him a kiss on the cheek. “You are going to go home with your parents and get the rest you need. I know you. If you come with me, you will just stay awake all night trying to make sure I'm safe."

"I need to be with you, Rayna."

"No," she said, placing her hand on his cheek, "you need to go home and take care of yourself. Get some sleep. I will be just fine."

"Yes, she will," Creed promised gruffly, stepping forward and clasping a hand on Ryder's shoulder. "I'll watch over her tonight, like I should have been doing all along. Forgive me?"

Ryder hesitated, looking from Creed to Rayna. "If anything happens to her…"

"Nothing is going to happen, little brother, I promise."

"And I will cover your shift at work tomorrow," Katy volunteered.

"It's your day off," Ryder protested weakly.

"When was the last time you had a day off?"

Not knowing how to respond to that, Ryder looked up into Rayna's eyes. "Promise me you will be okay." He knew it was unfair to make her promise him something she had no control over, but it did not stop him from asking.

"Everything is going to be just fine," she murmured, leaning over and kissing him softly on the lips. It was a sweet, soft kiss, and as much as he loved it, Ryder wanted so much more.

"I would like to keep you in the hospital overnight," the doctor said, laughing at the look

Ryder shot him, "but I know it will never happen. However, Ryder, you need to rest. Your body needs time to recuperate from everything you have put it through. It isn't going to happen overnight. Take a few days, let your family take care of you for once."

"I have to take care of the animals."

"I will take care of everything that needs done on the ranch," Caiden told them. "I don't have any animals in the clinic right now. I will close it down, and just work on an on-call basis until things are back to normal."

What exactly was normal? Ryder wondered, leaning weakly back against the pillows behind him.

"I can help Caiden," his father said.

"Not too much, you won't," Dr. Winninghoff responded. "I don't need you back in here too."

Ryder's father had suffered a mild heart attack a couple of years ago, and that was when Ryder took over everything with the ranch. Charles did the bookwork, but Ryder handled the rest. "I can handle it," Caiden said, straightening from the wall. "You can supervise, Dad." Everyone chuckled knowingly, because that was exactly what Charles would do.

Rayna smiled down at him, running her fingers through the unruly lock of hair covering his forehead again. "I need to get going now, Ryder, but stop worrying about me. I'm trained to take care of myself. I will be just fine."

"Do you need a job?" Katy grinned at her. "I know of one position that just opened up, and we were already actively searching for a couple of deputies. Plus, with me leaving in a few months, Creed is really going to need the help."

"You're leaving?"

"Let's just say I need to do a little investigating regarding some things in my past," Katy answered. "While I'm gone, we could use you here."

Ryder's heart skipped a beat as he waited for Rayna's response, and then it took off flying when she replied, "I will definitely keep that in mind."

After one last look at him, Rayna left the room. He watched her go, before turning to his family. "Keep her safe. I can't lose her again."

Chapter 27

The ride home was short, but Ryder was on Rayna's mind the whole way there. He was adamant that his family take care of her, and it warmed her heart that he cared for her the way he did. Her feelings for him had grown from the teenage crush of years ago into something so much more. Somehow, the man had managed to get past all of her defenses. She was so deeply in love with him, that she knew there was no way out. Now she just needed to figure out how to stay alive, so she could find out if he felt the same.

The minute Rayna walked into her house, she knew she was not alone. Acting on instinct, she grabbed her gun, ducking at the same time, barely missing the knife that embedded itself deep in the door behind her. He had finally decided to stop fucking with her, and was going to try and take her out. Screw that. She finally had something to live for. She would not be going down easily. Crossing the living room floor at a run, she jumped behind the loveseat, barely missing the knife that flew her way, sticking in the wall just above her head. So, the bastard preferred knives over bullets. That could be to her advantage. Making herself stay still, she listened intently, trying to pinpoint exactly where he was.

Everything happened so fast when she entered the house, that she didn't know for sure. He was either on the stairs, or in the dining room. From the angles of where the knives hit, she was betting on the stairs.

Knowing her best chance was to come at him fast and hard, Rayna rose quickly, spraying bullets at the stairs, before ducking behind the loveseat again. Excitement filled her when she heard at least one bullet hit its mark, as the intruder cursed loudly. "You fucking bitch," he yelled. "You will pay for that!"

Rayna grabbed the Glock 22 hidden in her boot. It was time to get serious. Instead of standing again, and giving him a clear shot, Rayna crouched low, running across the floor to the dining room, squeezing the triggers of both guns as she went. Another knife came at her. This one skimmed her arm, nicking it before sticking in the far wall. Rayna let out a hiss of pain as she rounded the corner, slamming her back up against the wall, breathing heavily. Carefully, she placed one of the guns on a shelf beside her. Removing her phone from her front pocket, she clicked on a button, pulling up the screen that held images of all of the rooms in her house. It was money well spent, she thought, stopping on one of the pictures. He'd gone back upstairs, and was sitting on the floor in her parents' old room. There was blood pouring from a wound in his thigh, and she could tell he was pissed off. He looked familiar, but even though she tried to zoom in on his face, she could not quite place him. The man quickly removed his shirt, tying it around his leg, over the wound. As she watched, he pulled a SIG from his belt. "I guess you like bullets after all."

The man stood, stumbling out of the bedroom and down the hall. "You can run, but you can't hide," Rayna murmured. She heard the creak on the third step down from the top, as he tried to creep down them. She knew every noise the house made. Had made it a point to study every little thing about it when she moved in. She was done playing. Her future with Ryder was on the line. The son of a bitch was going down.

Rayna knew the minute he hit the bottom step. She sat her phone down on the shelf, and picked up the 22. Raising both guns, she stepped around the door, standing in the entrance of the living room. Holding them steady on him, she snapped, "Who are you, and what the hell are you doing in my house?" After getting a clear look at him, she already knew the answer to both questions, but her intention was to distract him from the weapon he had pointed in her direction.

"You aren't as good as you think you are," he huffed, favoring his left leg. "That was a lucky shot."

"Oh, really?" One corner of her mouth turned up into a slow, easy grin.

“Yeah, you only figured out the one clue I left you. You only saw the doors. Someone better would have caught everything.”

“Everything?” she repeated, with a smirk. “You mean like the way you came into my house and messed with my magazines I had on the kitchen counter? Putting them in a different order than I left them? Or maybe the curtains in the bedroom that were drawn back, when I had them closed? Or how about the nice little surprise you left in my car? It was good, but not quite good enough. Took me awhile to find it, but I finally did. If you had taped the picture of my family just a little bit higher in the rear wheel well, I may not have seen it at all. Nice touch with the blood, by the way. Smearing it over our faces like that. Scary.” As his eyes filled with fury, she laughed. “Thanks for leaving me your DNA so that they can match it up when I take you in.”

“It’s not my blood,” he sneered, “and you aren’t that good!”

“Yes,” Rayna said confidently, “I am. Tell Diego, I’m waiting for the bastard.”

“Tell him yourself,” the man snarled, his finger tightening on the trigger of his gun.

Rayna jumped to the left, squeezing her 9mm twice, before falling to the floor. His bullet missed her by mere inches. She watched as he fell, his eyes opened wide in death. Slowly, Rayna rose, her hands still clutching both guns tightly, and walked over to stand above him. She knew who he was. She'd seen his mug shot several times. He was just one of many that Diego sent out to do his dirty work. "One less now," she muttered, kneeling beside him.

Seeing a phone peeking out of the front pocket of his jeans, she put the Glock 22 back in her boot, then reached over and grabbed it. It was time. Pulling up the caller ID, she looked at his last calls, smiling when she saw the number with the D.C. area code. Clicking on it, she put the phone to her ear and waited for it to be answered.

"Is it done?"

Rayna's face hardened when she recognized Diego's voice, and she grasped the phone tightly in her hand. "Oh, it's done," she replied darkly.

There was silence, and then, "Who is this?"

"You know who it is, Diego. You know exactly who I am." Glancing back down at the man who lay dead on her floor, she said, "Your move, asshole." Ending the call, she dropped the phone on the man's lifeless body.

Chapter 28

Diego Cortez slowly lowered the receiver from his ear, gritting his teeth in displeasure. Picking the phone up from his desk, he let out a roar as he threw it across the room, receiving no satisfaction when it hit the wall and fell to the floor. There was only one way he was going to be able to deal with the call he just received.

She had taken out one of his best men. They made a mistake thinking she was less than what she really was. Macey Fuller was good. Very good, if she could best Pedro Hernandez the way she had. Unless…maybe she'd had help? Maybe she wasn't in Serenity Springs alone?

Retrieving his cell phone from his pocket, he dialed a number he kept on speed dial now, and waited. Soon he heard a tentative voice on the other line answer, "Yes."

"I want everything you have on Macey Fuller, and why she is in Serenity Springs," he said.

"I don't have access to that information," was the soft response.

"I don't give a fuck how you get it," he snarled, "but you better have it to me by this time tomorrow, or that sweet little girl of yours is dead."

"I'll see what I can find out," she promised.

"You better," he muttered, before ending the call. Placing the phone back in his pocket, Diego hollered, "Nickolas, get in here!"

Soon the door opened, and a young man, his features resembling Diego's, stood in front of him. "Yes, Father."

"Pack your bags," he ordered. "We leave in the morning." Nickolas didn't ask any questions, as he turned to walk away. "And, Nick."

His son's shoulder's stiffened, but he did not look back. "Yes, Father?"

"Make sure and bring your gun."

His son left the room without a response, causing Diego to chuckle darkly. He knew Nickolas hated the business his dad ran, but the kid had no choice in whether or not to be a part of it. He was the son of the famous Diego fucking Cortez, and he would do whatever he was told.

Diego knew for a fact that the boy had never killed before. Well, he was sixteen years old now. It was time he became a man. Grinning cruelly, Diego decided, yes, Nickolas would be the one to pull the trigger and kill the woman who had become the bane of his existence. And, he would be there to watch to make sure his son followed through with his orders.

Chapter 29

Rayna stood in front of the Caldwell's door, her hand raised to knock. She hesitated, unsure if she should, or if it would be better to just turn around and go back home. There was no one following her right now, not with Diego's henchman gone, but she still worried about leading someone directly to the ranch.

It was late afternoon, several hours since her showdown with Hernandez…since she was forced to kill for the first time. Her hands were still shaking with the enormity of what she'd done. Her first and only call afterwards was to Assistant Director Talbot, then she sat and waited for the FBI to show up at her place. They removed the body and took her statement, not bothering to involve local law enforcement since Rayna was one of their own. They'd been at her house the majority of the day, and she was surprised when none of the Caldwells stopped by to ask questions.

After everyone left, Rayna lasted a full hour in her large, empty house before getting in her car to come see Ryder. She had nowhere else to go. No one else who cared for her the way he did. Rayna needed that right now, needed him. Taking a life was not an easy thing to do, no matter who the person was or what they may have done in their past. Pedro

Hernandez raped, tortured, and killed, but it did not make her feel any better. It bothered her that she'd taken a life, even if it was someone like him. It made her wonder how it would really feel if it came down to her or Diego in the end. There was no doubt that she would pull the trigger, but it might be harder to do than she'd originally thought.

Before she could decide whether she should actually knock or not, the door opened and Cara smiled gently at her. "Please, come in."

"I don't know if I should," Rayna admitted, haltingly, unable to stop the tears that slipped free. "I don't know if it's safe."

"Come here, child," Cara whispered, enfolding Rayna into her arms.

A sob left Rayna's throat before she could stop it. First one, then another, and another. "I'm sorry," she cried raggedly, "I hate that I dragged you all into this. If I could go back and change it all, I would."

"Ssshhh," Cara whispered, lightly stroking Rayna's back. "It's going to be okay, Rayna. Everything is going to be just fine."

"I could be putting you in danger just by being here."

"Didn't we already talk about this?" Cara questioned her softly. Tilting Rayna's head up until their eyes met, she said kindly, "You are always welcome here, Rayna Williams. Always, no matter the circumstances." Gently wiping the tears from Rayna's face, Cara gave her one last hug before guiding her into the house and closing the door behind them. "Have you eaten dinner?"

"No," Rayna said, shaking her head. She hadn't even eaten breakfast or lunch.

"Well, why don't you go check and see if Ryder is awake and ready for some food? I'll get something put together for the both of you." Rayna bit her bottom lip, pushing back more tears that threatened to fall, as she nodded in agreement. "He's up the stairs, first bedroom on the right," Cara told her, motioning toward the living room.

"Thank you," Rayna whispered. Crossing the room, she stopped at the bottom of the stairs to look back at the woman who still stood there gazing at her in concern. "Thank you, Mrs. Caldwell. Your kindness means so much to me."

"I think it's about time you started calling me Cara," Ryder's mom teased.

Returning Cara's smile with a wobbly one of her own, Rayna whispered thank you again before leaving to go find Ryder. The door was closed, and she knocked softly, but there was no response. Opening it, she stepped inside, closing it quietly behind her.

Ryder was asleep on the bed, the covers pulled up over his shoulders. He looked so peaceful. Unwilling to wake him after everything he'd been through, Rayna turned to go. Stopping with her hand on the doorknob, she bowed her head. She could not leave him. She needed him right now. Glancing back in his direction, she was surprised to see his eyes opened. He held out his hand to her, and she didn't hesitate. Moving to the bed, she removed first her 9mm, setting it on the end table, the Glock 22 quickly following. After kicking off her boots, she slid under the covers and curled up next to him. Resting her head on his shoulder, she let out a deep sigh of contentment.

"What happened?" he asked quietly.

"How do you know something happened?" she whispered.

"The other day you refused to step foot on this property, Rayna, afraid whoever was stalking you would follow. Now you are here in my bed."

"He's not a worry anymore," she told him, as her body began to tremble. The fact that she killed him remained unsaid.

Ryder gathered her close, nuzzling the top of her head with his chin. "Do you want to talk about it?"

"Not right now," she whispered.

"Rayna…"

"Please, Ryder. I can't. I just need you to hold me."

"Just tell me one thing," he finally said. "Are you safe?"

“For now,” she murmured, “until Diego sends somebody else, or comes himself.”

She felt his arms tighten around her, before he gently nuzzled her again, kissing her softly. “Then I suggest we both get some rest, so we are ready when they get here.”

Rayna felt herself slowly drift off to sleep, feeling safe, for now. Neither of them saw Cara peek in on them an hour later, a smile covering her face at the sight of her son resting peacefully, holding the woman she knew was meant for him.

Chapter 30

The man was moving slowly down the stairs, a knife in one hand and a gun in the other. An evil grin appeared when he reached the bottom and turned to face her. "You aren't as good as you think you are, Rayna Williams," he sneered.

A scream tore from Rayna's throat, and she jerked against the hands that held her down. She had to find her gun. Had to end this.

"Rayna, sweetheart," a voice crooned hoarsely, "I'm right here. No one is going to hurt you." Rayna stilled, her chest heaving as she fought to get her bearings. "That's it, baby. Come back to me. I will always protect you."

"Ryder." His name was a long breath on her lips. He was there. She was safe. Opening her eyes, she stared at the image above her until Ryder's handsome face came into view. Her body was shaking, her breathing labored. He held her wrists firmly, her arms out to her sides. There was no fear in his clear, blue eyes, only compassion and understanding.

"There you are," he said, a small smile teasing the corners of his lips. When she would have replied, he pressed his lips lightly against hers. A tear slipped out against her will, and he kissed it away. "We are going to get rid of those nightmares. I promise."

Tugging her arms from his grasp, Rayna did the exact opposite of what he probably thought she would do. She wrapped them around his neck, pulling him close, and held on tight. "I am so glad I have you," she whispered.

Ryder lay on his side, holding her snugly against him. "The feeling is definitely mutual." His hand moved up her back, then back down, before roaming lower still over the curve of her ass. A low moan left her when he pulled her into his straining erection.

They both jumped at the knock on the door, and Rayna let out a nervous laugh. She'd almost forgotten where they were, which could have been bad with the thoughts that were running through her head.

"Ryder," his mother called, "Is Rayna alright?"

"Yeah, she's fine," he hollered back. Leaning down, he placed a light kiss on the tip of her nose. "It was just a dream."

"Well, I have some breakfast ready if you are hungry. Come on down when you're ready."

Rayna blushed, ducking her head into Ryder's shoulder to hide her embarrassment. She was in his parent's house, she knew she was being disrespectful, but her body didn't seem to care. Ryder chuckled, "We'll be right there, Mom."

Rayna relaxed slightly when she heard Cara move away from the door, then let out a squeak when Ryder yanked back the covers, and smacked her butt playfully. "Ryder!"

He wiggled his eyebrows at her, then flipped her over onto her back on the bed. "Yessss?" He drew the one word out, as he slipped his hands under her shirt and slid it up just under her breasts.

"Stop that!" Rayna ordered, surprised at the giggles that slipped free when he rubbed his scratchy stubble of a beard over her belly. "Ryder," she squealed, when he not only did not stop, but began to tickle her sides. She squirmed around on the bed, trying to get away from him. She'd always been so ticklish, and she could not hold back her laughter.

Ryder's eyes were full of happiness, and it was a long while before he finally stopped torturing her. Pulling her arms above her head, he held her wrists in one hand. His eyes darkened with desire, as he leaned into her, claiming her mouth with his. She moaned, rising up to put her body flush against his, wanting to feel his skin against hers.

The sound of a horn honking outside tore them apart, and Ryder rasped, "We better get downstairs before mom sends up the cavalry."

Rayna sank reluctantly back down into the pillows, leaving the room with Ryder the furthest thing from her mind.

"Rayna…"

"What?" she whispered, her tongue darting out to wet her bottom lip as she gazed at his mouth.

"Woman, you are going to be the death of me," Ryder teased, his eyes alight with something more than just joy.

Rayna frowned, the reality of their situation coming back to her. "That's what I'm afraid of."

Ryder slid from the bed, and turned around holding out his hand. "Let's worry about all of that tomorrow," he suggested. "Today is our day. No bad guys, no fear of the unknown. Just us."

She stared at his hand, wondering what it would be like to spend a whole day with Ryder and not worry about who might be watching them, or trying to kill them. Wanting nothing more at that moment than to find out, Rayna reached out and placed her hand in his.

Later that morning after breakfast, a shower and a change of clean clothes from a bag she always kept in her car just in case she needed it, Rayna followed Ryder out of the house. "Are you sure you should be moving around like this, Ryder? I thought the doctor wanted you to get more rest?"

"I slept all day yesterday, and all night last night, sweetheart, I think that's more than enough rest."

"Well, if you fall on your ass, I'm not picking you back up," she piqued, skipping past him to the barn. Even though she knew Diego was still out there somewhere, she somehow felt free today. Ryder said it was their day, and as crazy as it might sound, she felt like he was right. It was going to be a good day, and nothing could ruin it.

Entering the dim building, she rushed over to Heaven and her mother where they stood in the stall the foal was born in. Full of excitement, she opened the door and stepped in, smiling when Heaven immediately came over to her. "Hey there, gorgeous," she murmured, "I've missed you."

"She's missed you too," Ryder said, leaning against the stall door, his arms over the top, a wide grin on his face.

Rayna's face flushed with pleasure, and she rubbed a hand gently down the foal's nose, and then her neck. "She probably doesn't even remember me."

"She remembers," Ryder promised, chuckling when Heaven bumped her head against Rayna's chest, begging for more attention.

"She's so beautiful," Rayna breathed in awe, her gaze wandering over the soft, shiny black and white coat.

"Yes, she is." Rayna looked back at Ryder, a question hovering on her lips. "What?"

She shrugged, looking back at the foal. "I just wondered why you kept the name Heaven," she admitted.

"Because you were right."

"I was?"

"She's just like the song." The words were spoken quietly, and with meaning.

Looking down into Heaven's stunning, dark brown eyes, Rayna's heart melted even more. And when Ryder started to sing softly, she could not keep the tears at bay. Closing her eyes, Rayna let his words wash over her, filling her with a love like she'd never felt before. She loved this man, more than life itself.

When the song was over, Rayna walked over to him, cupping his cheeks in the palms of her hands. "Ryder, you mean so very much to me," she whispered. It was the best she could do right now. Until her fight with Diego was finished, it would have to do.

Ryder covered her hands with his, turning to kiss first one palm, and then the other. "Me too," was all he said. They stood like that for several minutes before Ryder finally pulled back. "How about we go for a ride and have that picnic we missed out on the other day?"

"Sounds good to me."

Saying a quick goodbye to Heaven, Rayna went to the house and helped Ryder pack up some sandwiches and chips, along with apples for the horses and cherry pie for dessert. After saddling up Cochise and a pretty dark grey mare Ryder called Whisper, they rode west a few miles out until they came to a body of water. Stopping, they left the horses to nibble on the grass, and made their way close to the pond. Ryder placed a blanket on the ground beside it, and then took the lunch bag from Rayna motioning for her to sit.

They spent their lunch talking about anything and everything that came to mind, and when they were finished, they laid on the blanket, snuggling as they talked some more. Rayna had never felt so comfortable around anyone, and before she knew it, she was sharing her favorite memories of her family with him, things she never talked to anyone about.

Chapter 31

Ryder leaned back on one elbow, looking down at Rayna where she lay on the blanket beside him. She was so damn beautiful. Her dark hair was spread out around her, her brown eyes lit with joy as she recounted a story about when she was younger and she and Matty were camping outside by the barn alone. Unable to stop himself, he trailed a finger down the velvety soft skin of one arm, loving the way her full, pink lips curved into a smile laced with love for her brother. She was perfect, everything about her, and she was his.

"Tell me," he said curiously when her story was over, "if things had turned out differently, what do you think you would be doing now?

"What do you mean?" she asked, and he groaned at the way the tip of her tongue snuck out to wet her lips. She did that often, and it drove him fucking crazy.

"I never would have pictured you as an FBI agent," he told her honestly. "Actually, I never would have thought you would work in law enforcement at all."

"Me neither," she admitted. "I hated guns back then, and was afraid of the littlest things."

"Like?"

She looked away from him, out toward the water. “Anything and everything. I grew up knowing Diego was hunting us. I imagined him in every corner, under every bed. I was terrified of the dark, of any unfamiliar noise.”

“Really? I don’t ever remember you being scared when we spent time together.”

“I wasn’t thinking about Diego when I was with you,” she murmured.

“No?”

“No.” When she didn’t elaborate, he asked again, “So, what did you want to be when you grew up?”

Turning her head back to look at him, she smiled. “What did you think I would be?”

“A teacher,” he replied instantly. “You always had a book in your hand. I thought maybe you would teach English or Reading to elementary students someday.”

“Close,” Rayna said, glancing back out over the rippling water. “When I was younger, I did want to be a teacher, but that changed the older I got. Reading was my passion, and the more I read, the more I wanted to not only read my books, but to live in them as well. They made it so that I didn’t have to think about what was really going on in my life. I would come up with stories, spinning fairytales, and pretending I was the heroine. I was always going on an adventure, being saved by a knight in shining armor, falling in love."

"You wanted to write about the stories you wished you lived in?" he guessed.

A sad smile forming, she nodded, "Yes. I wanted to give some other child, one who might be going through something like I was, a chance to dream."

"You can still do that, Rayna" Ryder encouraged, leaning closer to her. "You can do anything you set your mind to, sweetheart, I know it."

"No, I can't," Rayna sighed, meeting his gaze again. "I don't have any fairytales in me anymore, Ryder."

"Then we need to make some," he whispered, capturing her lips with his. He refused to let her feel like she had no hope left. He wanted to show her how much she meant to him, how much he cared for her, and so much more.

Slipping his hand under her shirt, Ryder slid it over the soft skin of her belly, groaning low in his throat as he moved it up to cup her full breast, covered in silk. Rayna gasped as he slid his hand under the material, grazing her nipple with his thumb, arching into his hand, she cried, "Ryder!"

"I love it when you say my name like that," he rasped, licking at her neck as he squeezed her nipple lightly.

"Like what?" she moaned, her body trembling under his hands.

"Like I'm all you want. All you need." Ryder slid an arm around her shoulder, and lying down on his back, he pulled her over on top of him. Grasping her shirt in his hands, he slipped it up over her head and dropped it to the ground beside them.

Sitting up, Rayna straddled his hips, and slowly started to undo the buttons on his shirt. "That's because you are."

Ryder helped her get rid of first his shirt, then his boots and pants, her declaration ringing in his ears. He was all she needed. That was good, because he felt the same way about her. "Rayna." He wanted to tell her how he felt. That she was the first thing he thought about in the morning, and the last before he went to bed. That he never wanted to go another day without hearing her voice, and feeling her touch. That she lit up his world, and he was nothing without her. But, she covered his mouth with a finger, silencing him. "Not now," she whispered. "Not yet."

"Why not?"

"We aren't going to talk about why. Not today, Ryder. Today is our day, remember? I don't want to bring anyone or anything into it. It's just you and me."

"Nothing is going to change the way I feel," he told her, hoping she saw the truth in his words. "I mean it, Rayna. Nothing."

"Good," she said, removing her jeans and panties, and straddling him once again. Sliding her hands to the front clasp of her bra, she undid it, slipping it off, baring her breasts to him.

Grasping her hips, Ryder raised her up some, and brought her down slowly on his hard cock, groaning loudly when he was enveloped by her wet heat. "I love the way you feel," he rasped, arching his hips to bury himself further inside. Rayna rose, sliding up his cock, before falling slowly back down, pushing him in even deeper. Watching her, he nearly came when she brought her hands up to cup her own breasts, tilting her head back, and playing with her nipples. "Baby," he growled, tightening his hold on her hips, and increasing his pace, "that is so fucking hot."

Rayna lowered her head, looking at him with eyes wide with desire. "Feels so good," she moaned, letting go of her breasts to put her hands on his chest. Taking over, she adjusted her hips, and began to move faster and faster. "So close," she panted, "Ryder!"

Ryder slid his fingers over her head, grasping a handful of hair. Tightening his grip, he met her thrust for thrust, and soon was following behind her as she screamed his name when she came.

After a moment, Ryder loosened his grip on her hair, but tugged her down for a kiss, then held her close to his chest. "We should get our clothes on," she finally whispered.

"Why?" He lightly stroked a hand down her back, not wanting to let her go.

"What if someone is out there? Watching us?"

"There is no one around here but you and me," he promised, wrapping his arms around her and holding her close.

"But, what if there is?" Rayna insisted. "They could have a sniper rifle, and be watching us from anywhere."

"Then I would die a happy man," Ryder said, flipping her over onto her back, and covering her mouth with his before he started to move inside her again.

Chapter 32

Creed and Katy were waiting for them when Ryder and Rayna arrived back at the house later that afternoon. Creed was leaning against his truck, Katy sitting on the tailgate. Rayna could tell by the look on Creed's face that he had somehow found out about the day before. Not bothering to sugarcoat it, she dismounted from Whisper, dropping the reins, and placed her hands on her hips. "I didn't come to you when it was over because the FBI had jurisdiction. The man is dead and gone, and that is all that really matters, Sheriff."

She was aware of Ryder coming up beside her and placing a hand on the middle of her back in reassurance. Rayna leaned into his touch, her eyes locked on Creed. She had come into his town, stirred up trouble, and killed a man. He had every right to be pissed, even if it was an FBI case.

"I disagree," Creed replied, copying her stance, glaring down at her. "I was getting ready to leave the house last night, when my mother called to let me know that you were going to stay here."

"It was safe," Rayna said defensively. "I wouldn't have come otherwise."

"Rayna, that's not what I'm trying to get at." Creed removed his Stetson, raking a hand through his thick hair. “Look, I know I have been a jerk lately, and I apologize. It has nothing to do with you.”

“I know,” Rayna responded quietly. “You are just worried about your family.”

“Yes,” he agreed, replacing the Stetson, “but all of that changed yesterday.”

“How?”

Creed’s gaze left hers, going to his brother. “I realized exactly how much you have come to mean to Ryder,” he said. “I should have seen it sooner, but I was so busy trying to protect my family, that I missed the most important thing.”

“What’s that?” she whispered, stepping back slightly to lean into Ryder’s chest. He wrapped his arms around her, pulling her close.

A slow grin appeared on Creed’s lips, and he said, “You *are* family, Rayna.” Rayna teared up as Creed continued, “I should have been there for you yesterday, but it took awhile for me to pull my head out of my ass. I’m sorry. You should not have gone through what you did alone.”

“It was better that you weren’t there,” Rayna said, crossing her arms over her chest. “There is a good chance one of us would have been killed if you were.”

She felt Ryder’s hold tighten on her, and he muttered in her ear, “I think we better talk about this later.”

Tilting her head back, Rayna whispered, "If you want, but you won't like it."

"All I know is that your boss called and chewed me out because I obviously wasn't doing a good job assisting his agent. He said they came close to losing you, Rayna."

"Fuck," Ryder growled, burying his face in her neck. "I'm not leaving you alone again," he vowed. "I'm not letting you out of my sight."

"Don't worry, Ryder," Katy said, from where she now stood beside the sheriff's truck, "one of us will be with her at all times. That bastard won't get near her."

Rayna pulled away from Ryder, lifting up her hands, palms out. "You can't do that," she told them, in shock that they wanted to protect her the way they did, but knowing Diego would not show his face if they were around. "I'm here to do a job, and that job is to draw Diego to me and take him down. I work for the Federal Bureau of Investigations," she stressed, "they don't let just anyone in. I am fully trained, and I am good at what I do. I will be fine."

"We protect our own," Creed said, "that means you, Rayna."

Rayna felt a piece of her heart that had been broken for years begin to mend at that moment. She'd been without family for so long, but suddenly these people were stepping up and claiming her as one of their own. They did not seem to care that there was a price on her head. She was all that mattered to them, and they would fight for her. "It means so much to me that you would do this," she choked out, "but I will never be free of that bastard until he's behind bars. The only way for that to happen is to get him here, but he won't come if I have a house full of law enforcement."

"No," Ryder agreed, "but he won't be intimidated if it is just me, a cowboy."

Creed's eyes narrowed as he considered what Ryder said, before slowly nodding his head in agreement. "True." Looking him up and down, Creed demanded, "Are you sure you are up to it?"

"Yes." Ryder's response was quick and decisive, and before she knew it, they were putting the horses in their stalls and going to the bunkhouse to pack a bag for Ryder. It seemed he was coming home with her, and his siblings were going to take turns staking out her farm during the night from a distance where they would be able to help if needed. Knowing she would not be able to keep him away, and realizing her time at the Caldwell's place was quickly coming to an end, Rayna finally agreed to their plan. It would be safer for everyone if they left soon. Diego could already have someone else on their way to Serenity Springs, and as much as she enjoyed her time at the ranch, she did not want to lead any of her enemies there.

After saying goodbye to Charles and Cara, and thanking them for their hospitality, Rayna walked to her car, waiting for Ryder to put his bag in the back seat before sliding in the front. Taking one last look around, she got in the driver's seat and headed home, her perfect day with the man she loved was over.

That night in bed, Rayna cuddled close to Ryder, and quietly told him what happened to her the night before. She did not leave anything out, because she refused to lie to him, and omitting the truth was the same as a lie to her. When she was done, Ryder traced the Band-Aid on her arm, his body rigid against hers. "This is where the knife got you." It wasn't a question. He had seen the wound the night before, but hadn't asked any questions, probably because he knew she wasn't ready to talk about it.

"Yes," she said softly, covering his hand with hers, "but it was just a flesh wound. It doesn't even really hurt."

"And this one?" He moved his hand up, his fingers trailing over a scar on her shoulder.

"That's from the accident," she whispered. "once the car stopped rolling that night, a man appeared and fired at us. One went into each of us to make sure we didn't survive."

"But you did."

"Yes," she agreed, "I did."

Ryder laced his fingers with hers, kissing her hand and holding it against his cheek. "What happens when this is all over, Rayna?"

She knew what she wanted to happen. She would give everything up in Virginia in a heartbeat, to spend the rest of her life in Serenity Springs with him. But she could not make any promises she might not be able to keep. She did not have it in her. "Let's just concentrate on surviving," she murmured, "and worry about the rest later." Reaching down, she grasped the hem of her nightgown, and edged it up over her hips. She knew it was wrong to distract him with sex, but she could not talk to him about the future when she had no idea if she would even have one. Right now she just wanted to concentrate on the present, and the man who was sliding up her body and inside her, and making her believe in fairytales again.

Chapter 33

Lyssa opened the door to her apartment, a huge yawn slipping out. It was in the middle of the night, and she was just getting home from a couple of hours of fun with one of the cute cowboys she'd met at the diner. She knew it was wrong. She was there undercover, and her mission was to pass information from her contact in the agency to Rayna, not sleep with Clyde Walker who worked at the bar down the street. But she was so bored, so she went to see him at The Cavern, and one thing led to another.

The last few months had made her realize that she was not cut out for undercover work. She wanted to be where her skills were needed. She wanted to be out in the field, chasing and catching bad guys, not babysitting another agent while she waited for one to possibly show up. She had no idea how she'd drawn the short straw, but she hoped it was almost over.

The thought no sooner came to mind, than she was grabbed from behind, her door slammed shut behind her, and she was shoved up against the wall, a large knife held to her neck. "Hello little girl," a deep voice said, "we have been waiting for you."

Lyssa's eyes were wide in shock, and she struggled to free herself. The knife bit into her neck, and a trickle of blood ran down her skin. Her training kicking in, Lyssa brought her knee up, slamming it into the man's groin. He cursed loudly, lowering the knife just enough that she was able to butt her head into his. "You bitch!" he roared, bringing his arm back and letting his fist fly. Excruciating pain filled her when he connected with her face, and she screamed out in agony as she stumbled back into the wall.

There was laughter in the background, and then, "Bring her over here, dumbass, and tie her to the chair. Let's see what she will tell us."

The man in front of her grasped her chin tightly in his hand, squeezing her jaw, while he pounded her head back into the wall again and again. "Fuck that, we don't need to tie her down. She won't get the chance to do that again, and I want to play."

"I said bring her over here," the other guy ordered, obviously the one in charge.

Lyssa fought with all her might, but in the end she found herself tied to a chair, with nowhere to go. "Who are you?" she managed to gasp, her ears ringing loudly, and one eye nearly swollen shut. She had a bad feeling she knew exactly who they were, and now that she was bound to the chair, she was screwed. Why the hell had she thought she wanted to be in the middle of a lot more action?

"It doesn't matter who we are," the first man spat. "The only thing that matters is what I'm going to do with you after Frankie here talks to you."

"Frankie?" Oh shit, she was right. Every mob had to have a Frankie, and this one was Frankie Barker, Diego's main muscle. This was not good. The man was known by many for his torture skills. He knew how to inflict pain like no other.

Sitting down next to her, Frankie reached out and wrapped a blonde curl around his fingers. "What's a pretty young thing like you doing working for the FBI?" he wondered out loud. "I could think of a lot better things for you to be doing."

"Like what?" she muttered, even though she told herself to be quiet.

"Like sucking my cock," the other man grumbled.

"Ignore Rocky here," Frankie said, slowly letting the curl slide from his finger. "He gets a little excited sometimes."

Rocky, she thought as she turned to get a good look at the other man out of her good eye. Rocky Masters, famous for using his fists to mutilate and murder. She had definitely fucked up visiting Clyde for some fun, instead of staying home with her gun close and ready. Now the damn thing was in her purse over by the door, and she was tied to a motherfucking chair with nowhere to go. "I have no idea what you are talking about," she finally spit out through clenched teeth, the pain in her head overwhelming. "I'm just a waitress."

Frankie pulled a small notebook from his pocket and flipped it open. "Alyssa Monroe Taylor, age twenty-five, height five feet, six inches, weight one hundred thirty pounds. Never been married, no children. Lives at 213 Lily Street in Virginia. Father passed away from cancer ten years ago, mother lives with her sister in Florida." Stopping, he looked at her. "Do I need to go on?"

Lyssa grimaced when she swallowed some of the blood from a cut on the inside of her mouth before responding, "She sounds like she has an interesting life. My name is Melissa Timmons. I'm twenty-three. I never made it to college. Both of my parents are dead."

"Nice try, little Lyssa, but I have pictures. Would you like to see?" Reaching into another pocket, Frankie pulled out two pictures and held them up for her to look at. One was of her mother in Florida, walking down by the beach by herself. The other was of herself with her mother, from when she'd graduated college. The beach photo was from a bookcase in her living room. The college one was from the dresser in her bedroom. The bastards had been in her house.

Fury filling her, she raised her head to look at Frankie. "Fuck you," she spat.

Frankie backhanded her, then grabbed a fistful of her hair, yanking her head back. She sat paralyzed in fear when she got her first glimpse of what death looked like in his black, soulless eyes. She knew then that there was a very real chance she was going to be with her father in Heaven before the night was over.

Chapter 34

A slow, cocky grin spread across Nate's face as he held the door open for a couple of women who were leaving the diner. "Ladies," he said, tipping his hat in their direction. They giggled, casting flirtatious looks his way, hope shining in their eyes. Walking into Mac's, he let the door slide shut behind him. He wasn't interested in whatever they had to offer. There was only one woman on his mind lately, and she was keeping her distance since their time in his cabin.

After greeting some of the other patrons he'd gotten to know lately, he made his way up to the counter and took a seat. "Hey there, Miss Dottie," he drawled, taking off his hat and setting it on the stool next to him, "how about a cup of coffee and one of your breakfast specials this morning?"

"Coming right up," she responded immediately, although she looked a little anxious and upset.

Nate waited until she'd hollered the order back to the kitchen before asking, "What's wrong, sweetheart? You look a little worried about something."

Dottie frowned, the first one he'd ever seen pass over her normally happy features, and she began to fidget. Playing with the bangle bracelets on her arm, she stared at them as she moved them up and down her wrist. "I'm just busy," she finally replied, seeming to come out of her stupor.

Nate glanced around the diner, searching for Lyssa, who was actually the reason he stopped by in the first place. She was supposed to check in this morning with the field office, and pass on whatever information they had to him. "Hey, where's that pretty little waitress at," he teased, winking at Dottie. "I was hoping to maybe share my coffee with her this morning."

Dottie's lips tightened into a thin line, and she straightened her shoulders. "I honestly don't know. She was supposed to be here at five o'clock this morning, but no one's seen her. I know she went out last night, but it just isn't like her not to show up for her shift."

Dread began to creep up Nathan's spine, but he shot Dottie a teasing grin. "Has anyone gone to check on her? Maybe she just slept in after one too many drinks?"

"I called her, but it went straight to voice mail. It's just not like Melissa not to show up. She hasn't missed a shift since she started here." Someone across the room hollered Dottie's name, and she told them she would be right over. Patting his hand lightly, she said, "Let me get your breakfast for you, young man. That's enough worrying about Melissa. I'm sure she will be around soon."

Nathan had a gut feeling that wasn't true. Something was very wrong. Standing, he reached out and pulled on one of Dottie's curls, making her smile. "I need to get going ma'am. Do you think you could have that food boxed up for me? I'll eat it at the ranch."

"Of course! Give me just a minute."

Taking out his cell phone while he waited, Nathan discreetly sent a text to Agent Kayla Donaldson asking if Lyssa had checked in that morning. They were to keep all contact with the agency to a minimum unless it was an emergency, but right now he was declaring this one. It was not long before he got his response. *No.*

Fuck. Not bothering to wait for Dottie to return, Nate pulled out a twenty and dropped it on the counter before retrieving his hat and quickly leaving the diner. Dialing 911, he ran down the sidewalk, skirting around the corner to the back alley. "911 Emergency, how may I direct your call?"

"This is the FBI. Transfer me to Sheriff Creed Caldwell now!" he ordered roughly as he scanned the back of the building. Melissa's apartment had outside access only, and the steps leading up to it were in plain sight of anyone watching. He did not have a choice, he was going up.

Nathan was taking the steps two at a time when he heard, "Creed Caldwell."

"This is Special Agent Nathan Brentworth with the FBI, Sheriff. I'm over at the diner, and I need backup, fast."

"Talk to me."

"Another agent hasn't checked in. She's never late."

"Melissa."

He wasn't surprised that Creed knew exactly who he was talking about. He'd done his homework, and he knew the Sheriff was good at his job, and someone he could go to at a time like this. "Yes. Dottie said she didn't show up for work, and she hasn't been able to get a hold of her."

"I'm coming up the side of the building," Creed warned him. "I have two of my deputies with me."

"These guys aren't amateurs," Nathan warned him. "My guess is, if they have been here, they are long gone. But, it's better to be safe than dead."

"I agree."

Nathan waited at the top of the stairs, watching out for the others as they got into position. The deputies stopped, one on each corner of the building, continuously scanning around them. Creed ran lightly up the stairs, his gun drawn, and stood to one side of the door.

Nathan tried the door, and wasn't surprised to find it unlocked. Holding a hand up to stop Creed from going forward, he quickly checked the edges for any kind of wire. Vinnie Harris was known for his bomb making skills, and Diego Cortez never went anywhere without him. After a moment, Nathan grasped the doorknob and pushed the door open, crouching low, gun out in front of him. Creed was on his heels, and they made quick work of clearing the area before stopping outside the only closed door in the apartment. There was blood everywhere, so Nathan was not surprised at what he found when they entered the bathroom.

Lying in the bathtub, was his fellow agent. Her body was broken and bloody, her clothes shredded scraps of material barely covering her body. Deep cuts scored her flesh, and her skin was marred with dark bruises.

Quickly crossing the room, Nathan knelt beside her still form. Placing his fingers over the pulse on her neck, he closed his eyes to concentrate, praying he would feel it beating. There it was, very light, but it was there. Suddenly, Lyssa's eyes fluttered, and then opened slightly. "It's me, Lyssa," he said quickly, afraid she might think he was one of Cortez's men. "It's Nate."

"Nate." His name was just a whisper on her lips, so faint he almost didn't hear it.

"Yes, Lyssa, it's Nate. Hold on, honey. Help is coming." He could hear Creed on the phone in the background barking orders for an ambulance, and he prayed they got there in time. She was fading fast, and he was afraid if he lost her now, there would be no coming back from this for her.

"Nate," she breathed again. "Tried."

"Lyssa, look at me," he ordered. "Look at me!"

Her eyes closed again, and she whispered, "Had to tell them so they would stop. Had to."

Oh shit. "You had to tell them what, Lyssa?" A loud gasp left her throat, then another. "Lyssa!" he yelled, "what did you tell them?"

Her eyes opened into small slits, and she rasped, "Rayna. Ryder. New Hope."

"Sir, sir you need to step back. We need to get to her."

Nathan rose in stunned silence, not fighting the arms that moved him out of the bathroom. They had broken her. She had spilled everything. *Harper!*

"You go to Harper," Creed said, dialing another number on his cell. "I'll have my sister and one of my deputies meet you out there."

"They are going after Rayna," Nathan said, knowing the bureau would expect him to protect her. "And your family."

"You let me worry about my family and Rayna. You get to Harper."

Not bothering to argue, Nathan left the apartment, heading for his truck at a dead run. He knew Rayna was supposed to be his first priority, but right then he didn’t care. Let them fire him. He was choosing Harper.

Chapter 35

Harper Daley swore loudly, dropping the pipe wrench on the counter and barely resisting the urge to kick her kitchen cabinet. The drain to the sink was clogged. Nothing would go down no matter what she did. Instead of asking for help, once again she was trying to fix it herself.

"Why do I have to be so damn stubborn?" she muttered to herself, placing her hands on her hips and taking a deep breath, immediately wishing she hadn't. The kitchen still reeked of burnt toast from breakfast, even though all of the windows in the room were wide open.

On her ranch, the children helped with the cooking, cleaning, and they took turns taking care of the animals. Normally it was a good idea, but sometimes, like this morning, it pushed her limits. However, she was a firm believer in teaching them the importance of responsibility so they could survive on their own after turning eighteen. When the children arrived, the majority of them did not know how to boil water, do laundry, and had never even seen a riding lawnmower before, much less actually mowed with one. By the time they left New Hope Ranch, they could not only do all of that, but way more. And she was proud of each and every one of them.

At the sound of a car in her driveway, Harper walked over to the window to glance out. A black, four-door Sedan stopped in front of the house, and two men got out. One was very large and intimidating. She could see the hard glint in his eyes even from this distance. The other one wasn't quite as big, but still had a menacing look about him. A feeling of foreboding filled her chest when she saw they were both packing. They did not look like law enforcement, more like the thugs she used to know from the city. Had her past finally caught up with her? That didn't make sense. Why would they just now be tracking her down after all of these years? No, it couldn't be Julio's men.

Something wasn't right though, and she was going to have to face them alone. Henry was in Dallas picking up some things for the horses, the children were all at school, and she'd seen Nate leave a couple of hours ago.

Deciding she needed some kind of reinforcement in case this meeting was to go bad, Harper ran quickly to her office in the back of the house. Unlocking her large safe that was kept hidden in the back closet, she quickly removed a handgun, followed by a rifle. *Maybe it was a good thing she normally relied only on herself*, she thought, making sure both were loaded before shoving the revolver in the waistband of her jeans at her back. Picking up the rifle, she jumped at the ringing of the front doorbell. Screw that. She had no idea who these men were, but they would meet her on her terms.

Harper thought briefly of calling Nate, but she knew there was no time. Besides, what could he do? She just thanked God that the children were away. If anything were to happen to any of them, she would never forgive herself.

Opening the window in the office, Harper slipped through, dropping lightly to the ground. Grasping the rifle tightly, she stayed close to the house as she rounded the corner and moved up the side. Measuring the distance between the house and the barn, she thought briefly of darting into it to find a place to hide until they left. The only thing that stopped her was the thought of one of the children coming home and the men still being there.

"It doesn't look like anyone's around," one of the men said, his voice closer than she would have liked.

"The door is unlocked. They're here."

"I don't know, some of these country bumpkins leave everything unlocked. Idiots."

The voice was getting closer and closer, and Harper knew if she didn't make a move soon, she wouldn't be the one in control. Screw that, she was always in control. Stepping out from around the corner, she raised her rifle and leveled it on the man who stood just a few feet from her looking into the living room window. “Can I help you boys with something?”

They turned toward her, the larger one at the front door, the other stepping back from the house to face her squarely, his hand moving for his gun. “I wouldn’t do that if I were you,” she said, cocking her head to the side, a slow grin spreading across her face. “I can outshoot any man in this town. If you grab that gun, you won’t have it for long.”

“Now, ma’am,” he replied, holding his hands out in front of him, palms up. “We aren’t here to hurt you. I’m Rocky Masters with the Federal Bureau of Investigations. This here is my partner, Mr. Barker. We just need to talk to you about a wanted fugitive that we think is hiding out on your land.”

“Oh, really?” Harper raised an eyebrow, easily detecting the lies flowing from his mouth. “Then you won’t mind showing me your badges.”

“Look,” the other man interrupted in irritation, “we don’t have time to show you anything. This man is dangerous. He’s killed before, and could kill again. You may know him as Nate Burrows.”

Harper flinched slightly at the name, but her expression hardened considerably. She had already figured out that there was more to Nate than met the eye, but there was no way in hell the man was avoiding the law. She was a good judge of character, always had been, and Nate Burrows was a decent man. “Bullshit.”

“Ma’am.”

“Ma’am me again and I will put a bullet in you,” Harper warned. “I don’t know who the hell you are, but I do know that you are not with the FBI. I’ve dealt with the FBI before, and I have dealt with assholes like you. Now, you have ten seconds to get in your car and get the hell off my property, or you are going to be visiting our county jail, with a stop at the hospital on the way, instead of standing here exchanging pleasantries with me.”

The one called Rocky went for his gun first. It barely cleared the holster before she squeezed the trigger of her rifle and he dropped to the ground, his hand covering a hole in his side. Pulling the revolver from her jeans, she aimed it at Barker. “Give me a reason,” she growled. “I have had one fucked up morning, and putting you on the ground by your friend here would make it so much better.”

The man’s gaze went from Harper, to Rocky, and then past her to look at something out by the road. She did not turn around, knowing he would take advantage of the situation if she did. Hearing the sirens in the distance, along with a vehicle coming down her driveway, Harper grinned. “I guess it is off to jail with both of you after all.”

A truck pulled to a stop in front of the house, and Nate opened the door, jumping out. “Don’t even think about it," he growled when Barker reached for his gun. "After what you did to my partner, I will tear you the fuck apart."

Partner? "These boys decided to drop by and say hi this morning, Nate. They seemed to want to play some, but I'm just not in the mood for games."

"Me neither," Nate snarled, walking up to the big guy, and letting a fist fly. "She was just a kid, you bastard. A fucking kid!" Harper watched in shock as Nate slammed the other man up against the house, quickly removing his gun and two hidden knives, before slapping cuffs on him. Throwing him to the ground beside his buddy, Nate came over to stand by Harper. They stood in silence until Deputy Katy Caldwell arrived, all the while Harper was trying to figure out what the hell had just happened.

Chapter 36

Cara Caldwell filled the kitchen sink with soapy water, before submerging the large frying pan in it. She, Charles, and Caiden had just finished breakfast, and she was cleaning up while the men went to the barn to feed the horses. Afterwards, she and Charles were going to run into Dallas to get some things they needed. Her husband also promised her dinner and a little shopping for their granddaughter. She wanted to get Cassie a couple of new outfits for school.

Lost in thought, Cara stared out the window, smiling when she caught a glimpse of the new foal playing in the corral next to the barn. Heaven, what a beautiful name for the sweet filly. Although, she had a feeling Heaven wouldn't be at their ranch for long. She didn't foresee Ryder living there much longer either, even though she knew he would continue to run it. His heart belonged to Rayna now, and Cara was sure he would end up moving in with her soon. She had been so worried about him ever since the Johnsons passed away years ago. He changed, closing in on himself, and only showing everyone what he wanted them to see. When Rayna came home, he began to show signs of his true self again, a much happier one. There was no doubt in Cara's mind that Rayna was the one for her son.

Cara's mind turned to her son Justice. His time in the military would be up soon, but she knew that he was debating on re-enlisting, even after being held captive for months oversees. After recuperating at home with them, Justice went back to work, and she wasn't sure where he was right now. The government sent him on classified missions, the need to know kind. As his mother, she didn't need to know. She did not have that right. Cara understood though, and never pushed Justice for answers. As much as she wanted her son home, if his heart was with the military, she would stand by him. She would always encourage her children to follow their dreams. If that was what he was doing, then who was she to stand in his way?

Now, Linc was a different story. That boy was *not* following any dream on the rodeo circuit. Even though he may have enjoyed the rush of riding broncs when he was younger, life on the back of a bull was not something Linc ever wanted to do for the rest of his life. She knew her children well, and that boy was definitely hiding something from them.

Her sweet girl, Katy, would be leaving them soon. Although her daughter loved Serenity Springs, there had always seemed to be something missing in her life. Cara would do whatever she could to help her figure out what that was. It would be selfish of her not to. Yes, soon three of her six children would be gone.

Rinsing off the pan, Cara picked it up to dry, glancing back out the window again as she wondered if Charles was about ready to head out. Her eyes narrowed when she saw someone skirting around the barn, scanning the area around him. He was dressed in a dark tee-shirt, black jeans, and black boots. She'd never seen the man before, and she gasped when she saw him remove a gun from his back, holding it down next to him as he began to slowly creep toward the open barn doors.

Her husband and son were in that barn. She thought Caiden had his gun with him, but she knew Charles was unarmed. She watched the man stealthily making his way forward, and a deep anger filled her. She was so tired of the ones she loved being threatened.

Running to her husband's office, Cara opened the top drawer of Charles's desk and retrieved the key to the gun case. Soon, she was carrying a loaded pistol as she made her way out to the barn the man had just entered. She could hear voices inside, and could make out the authority in her husband's tone as he told the man to lower his weapon.

At the sound of a gun being fired, Cara did not hesitate. She ran into the barn, her pistol held high. At the sight of her husband on the ground and the man standing over him, his gun aimed at her son, Cara pointed the pistol and squeezed the trigger. No one messed with her family.

Cara watched as the gun slowly slipped from the man's fingers, and he collapsed to the ground. "Call an ambulance," she told Caiden, quickly closing the distance between herself and her husband. Her husband was now sitting up against the barn watching her, a look of pride in his eyes. There was no blood that she could tell, but she looked him over more than once to make sure. "Are you okay, Charlie?"

He chuckled softly, "I'm just fine, Cara girl," he said, pulling her into his arms. "Thanks to you, I'm just fine."

Chapter 37

Ryder watched as Rayna ended the call, putting the phone back in her pocket before turning to face him. "Was that my brother?" he asked.

"Creed," she confirmed, her eyes snapping in anger. "Diego's made a move."

"Tell me."

"He got to one of the agents that came to Serenity Springs with me," she ground out.

"Melissa?" The waitress from the diner. It had to be.

Rayna looked at him in surprise, "How did you know?"

"It was her?"

Rayna nodded, walking over to the loveseat and sitting down. "They found her in her apartment above the diner. It's bad, Ryder. They are taking her to the hospital now, but they don't know if she is going to make it."

"This is *not* your fault, Rayna." Ryder walked over and sat down beside her, taking her hand in his. "I know what you are thinking, but this is not your fault. Melissa was doing her job."

"Lyssa," Rayna rasped, her hand squeezing tightly to his. "Her name is Lyssa. She's young, one of the newer recruits. This was her first undercover mission, and now she is in the hospital fighting for her life because of me."

"No," Ryder insisted, "it is not because of you, Rayna. It is because of her job. If she wasn't here with you, Lyssa would be somewhere else, doing the same job." He knew nothing he said would matter right now, but he could not stand to see the self-loathing in her eyes. Sliding an arm around her waist, he pulled her close. "What else?" he asked. He knew there had been more to the conversation than Lyssa.

"They broke her, Ryder. By the time they were done, she told them everything she knew to try and stop the torture and pain." Lifting sad eyes to him, she said, "Everything about me. About Nathan, the other agent here in town who has been working at New Hope Ranch. About you and your family. Everything."

"Fuck!"

"Nathan was the one who found Lyssa, and called for help. He's on his way back to New Hope Ranch, and Katy is going to meet him there."

"My family?"

"Creed was calling Caiden next to warn him, and then he was going to come here, but I told him not to."

"Good idea," Ryder agreed. She looked at him in surprise. "Diego is not stupid. He will never show his face if my brother is here."

"That's why I told him to wait." Rayna looked down, inhaling deeply before saying, "Ryder, I want you to leave. I want you to go home and make sure your family is safe. They are so important, and they need you."

"*You* are important," Ryder said, tilting her head up so their eyes met. "You are important, Rayna Williams. Caiden will take care of my family. I am staying with you."

Rayna closed her eyes, nodding in agreement. "That's what I figured you would say, but I had to try." Placing a hand on his cheek, she said, "I need you to make yourself scarce. If he sees you here with me, then he may not show himself."

As much as he did not want to leave her side, Ryder knew she was right. Sliding his fingers into her hair, he held her still as he pressed his lips to hers. "I'll go, but I won't be far."

She placed two fingers over his mouth, and smiled gently. "Don't tell me where you will be. I don't want to be looking for you, and possibly give your position away."

When her fingers slipped away, Ryder leaned down and gave her one last kiss. "I won't be far," he promised again, before standing and leaving the house without a backward glance. He knew if he looked just one more time, he wouldn't be able to walk away.

Getting into his truck, Ryder left the farm, driving a couple of miles, before turning right on a dirt road and backtracking to Rayna's place. Grabbing a shotgun from behind the seat, Ryder left his truck less than a mile from her house in a secluded area, and ran quickly on foot back to the farm, praying he wasn't too late. He was hoping that Diego would follow his normal pattern of waiting to show his hand. He knew the minute he arrived at the farm that it wasn't going to happen this time, as he watched a young man walk up to Rayna and pull out a gun.

His eyes on them, he almost missed the man who slipped into the barn. As much as he wanted to go straight to Rayna, he knew that he needed to trust her to handle the situation on her own. Not only was she trained for it, but it was what she would want. If the man who went into that building was Diego, he was a much bigger threat than the kid.

After one last look at the woman who meant more to him than life itself, Ryder turned and ran to the barn, following the man inside.

Rayna sat in the gazebo, gazing out over the fields to the north of her, waiting. She had just heard from Nathan that Harper was fine. The woman successfully captured two of Diego's men on her own, and they were trying to cut a deal with Nathan now. One of them ratted out the fact that their boss was in Serenity Springs. It was all they'd given up so far, but she was sure there was more to come.

Her phone vibrated and she looked down to see a brief text from Creed. One more of Diego's men were captured at the Caldwell ranch. That one refused to talk.

Rayna knew Diego couldn't be far away. She was positive that if he sent men to New Hope Ranch and the Caldwells, then he was close by watching her. The smart move would be to attack all three places at once, and Diego was very intelligent. He would make his move soon.

What she did not expect was to hear the sound of a young man's voice instead of Diego's. "My father sent me to kill you."

Rayna turned to look at the teen standing beside her, a gun raised, his arm outstretched and trembling. The boy resembled Diego, with dark hair and eyes. Even his facial features were almost identical, except for the scar that ran from his temple to just below his cheekbone. "Nickolas," she said softly, her heart breaking at the pain and fear in his eyes. "You don't have to do this." She watched as he walked around the gazebo, then entered it with her.

"Yes, I do," he whispered, his lips barely moving, "He's watching. He's always watching."

The son of a bitch had ordered his own son to kill her. He couldn't even do it himself. "How old are you, Nickolas?" She knew, of course. She knew everything about Diego's family, what was left of it. His father was dead, as was his mother. Nickolas was from one of his mistresses. He had two daughters too, but they meant nothing to him, he only wanted his son. He wanted to mold the boy into a replica of himself, but it was not working. From what she knew, Nickolas was a dreamer, a writer, and an artist. He may be trained in the arts of exacting excruciating pain and murder, but he'd never actually killed before. She'd watched him for years, discovering the boy had a heart, unlike his father. A part of her had always hoped that he would be able to break away from the cruel man someday.

"Sixteen," he answered, his gun slowly beginning to lower.

"Don't do that," she said softly.

"What?"

"Raise that gun back up, pointed at me." When he looked at her in confusion, Rayna whispered, "I know you aren't going to hurt me, Nickolas. You aren't a murderer. But, you need to make it look like you are going to for your father."

"If I don't, he's going to kill me. He says I'm worthless to him if I can't pull a trigger."

"Maybe worthless to him, but I believe you to be a lot stronger than he thinks." Never looking away from Nickolas, Rayna called out to the man she knew could not be far. "What's wrong, Diego? You send your son to do your dirty work? Or maybe you know you can't best me yourself?" Hoping that if she pissed him off enough, he would show himself, she went on. "Why don't you come and face me like a man, instead of the coward I know you are?"

"What are you doing?" Nickolas muttered.

"Keeping you safe," she responded, rising slowly. If someone was going to die today, she did not want it to be him.

"Why?" The look in his eyes said it all. He'd never known anyone to care about him before, and rejected the idea that someone could now. He never had anyone to look out for him, and did not understand why someone he was sent to kill would want to.

"Because you are better than this, Nickolas. Better than him." Taking a step forward, Rayna said, "Trust me." Moving quickly, she grabbed the gun, sweeping his feet out from under him so he fell with her to the ground just as a bullet whizzed by his head. "Stay down," she ordered, dropping his weapon and retrieving her own. Diego was close, but where? Very carefully, Rayna raised her head over the enclosed lower half of the gazebo, quickly scanning the area before ducking back down. Shit, there were four of them, and they were slowly closing in on her. "How many are with you?"

"What?"

"How many men, Nickolas?" she spat out, removing her Glock 22 from her boot and mentally counting how many bullets she had.

"There were ten, including myself and my father. But, three went somewhere else when we came here."

Two at New Hope Ranch, one at the Caldwells, four coming toward her now. That meant there were still two more men out there somewhere. "No matter what happens, no matter what you hear, you stay down, Nickolas," she ordered roughly.

"What are you going to do?"

Determination glinted in her eyes when she replied, "Survive."

Chapter 38

After following the man into the barn, Ryder watched him walk to the other side of the barn and set something on the ground, before kneeling down beside it. Ryder was just about to make his move, when another man entered the building. Quickly hiding in one of the darkened corners, Ryder listened as the two began to discuss how far away they would need to be from the barn when the bombs they planted were detonated. It did not take long for him to realize that neither of them were Diego. That meant he was still out there, and there could be more of his henchmen with him.

"Let's get the hell out of here, man. I don't want to be standing here when this pile of crap falls in."

The man on the ground messing with the wires on the bomb didn't bother to turn around. "Go ahead, you chicken shit. We still have five minutes. I need to get this one just right."

"You are one crazy fucker, Vinnie." Shaking his head, he stood there grumbling about idiots with death wishes.

Ryder had no idea what was going on outside with Rayna, but he was done sitting there waiting to find out. Fear for his woman had Ryder stepping out into the open, his gun raised. “Hello, boys,” he drawled. “Is this a private party, or can anyone join?”

The one that was standing looked at him in surprise, hesitating a moment too long before going for his gun. Ryder put a bullet in his hand, making him drop the gun, cradling his hand as he screamed, “I’ll kill you! I will fucking kill you!”

Ryder’s gaze was on Vinnie now. The man didn’t move away from the bomb beside him. He picked up two wires, and turned to look at Ryder with a crazy ass grin on his face. Slowly, he started closing the distance between the wires, a psychotic glint in his eyes. Ryder turned and ran, just clearing the barn doors when the first bomb went off.

At the sound of a loud explosion, Rayna stood, guns aimed at where she’d seen the men before. She was able to get four shots off before dropping to the ground again to avoid the bullets coming her way. She was sure she’d hit two of the men, but the other two were still coming. Taking a deep breath, she peeked over the side of the gazebo, her eyes meeting the surprised gaze of a man just a few feet away. He grinned, raising his gun, but he was too late. Her bullet hit right between the eyes, before she ducked down again.

Resting her back against the wall, she glanced down at where Nickolas lay huddled in a ball, his body shaking in fear. “It’s almost over,” she promised him. “We are going to get through this.”

“I’ve been looking for you for a long time, Macey Fuller.” His voice rang out, deep and intimidating.

“There is no Macey Fuller here,” she responded angrily. “You killed her with the rest of her family years ago.”

Diego laughed harshly, and she looked up in shock to see him standing before her at the entrance of the gazebo. “I knew he didn’t have it in him.” Diego spat, motioning toward Nickolas, his eyes dark with fury, “He is too much like his sniveling mother. I had to put her down, and I will do the same with him after I deal with you.”

When Nickolas made a move to stand, she shook her head, “Don’t.”

“He’s going to hurt you,” Nickolas protested. Ignoring her, he rose, his gun pointed down to the ground at his side. “I can’t let that happen.”

The boy wanted to help her. His father was an evil man, a killer, but his son was a savior.

“Isn’t that fucking sweet,” Diego snarled. “My son finally grows a pair. Unfortunately it’s too late.”

Suddenly there was another loud explosion, and Rayna made the mistake of turning her head to watch in horror as her barn caved in, falling to the ground. *Ryder!* Where the hell was he? *Please don't let him be in the barn*, she prayed, *please God.* Her eyes on the destruction in front of her, she cried out in surprise when a shot rang out. Someone slammed into her, knocking her to the floor, and smacking her head into the bench.

Nickolas's body covered hers, as he tried to protect her from his father. Moaning in pain, Rayna struggled to push him off her, refusing to allow him to shield her. Her eyes widened in shock when blood dripped down from his shoulder onto her face. "Nickolas!"

"One down, one to go."

Rayna froze, realizing Diego was about to enter the gazebo with them. She'd lost her 9mm when they fell, and couldn't reach her other gun, even though she could see it just a few feet away.

"Take it," Nickolas rasped, pushing his gun into her hand.

Her fingers curled around the revolver, and she gripped it tightly. "Hold on," she whispered, "I'm going to get you help, Nickolas, just hold on."

"I've been waiting so long for this," Diego said, stepping into the Gazebo. "Now that it's come to an end, I find myself almost wishing I didn't have to kill you."

"It's not over yet, asshole," Rayna sneered, aiming at his kneecap and pulling the trigger. The shot went high, but she was satisfied when he yelled out, grabbing the railing to hold himself up. Rolling Nickolas off her, Rayna rose to her knees. Pointing the gun at Diego, she spat, “I’ve waited years for this, you bastard.” There was another loud boom, and she could hear the rest of the barn falling in, but Rayna only had eyes for the man in front of her. “You took everything from me, and now I’m going to take everything from you.”

“What? My son? He is nothing to me.”

“No, family is not what is important to a man like you, Diego. Power is. Wealth, material things, your empire. That’s what you consider important, and that is what I’m taking.”

“You can try,” Diego replied with a short laugh, “but once I get rid of you, I have a plane waiting to take me anywhere I want to go, and I’m taking my empire, as you call it, with me.”

“What makes you think you are leaving Serenity Springs a free man?” Rayna asked, her voice never wavering. “I didn’t bring you here, just to lose you again.”

“You didn’t bring me anywhere!”

“That’s where you are wrong. It was my idea to come here. I thought it would be easier to draw you out in the open, and I was right.”

“Did you think I didn’t know that?” Diego scoffed. “I have ties in the FBI. I have them everywhere. The only thing I didn’t know, until yesterday, was who was helping you. But, we found your Lyssa Taylor, at a diner in town. And although it took hours, and a lot of persuasion, sweet Lyssa led us to your other agent, Nathan Brentworth, on a ranch not far from here."

"And both of them are just fine," Rayna told him. Lyssa might not make it, but he didn't need to know about that. "Your men, on the other hand, are in custody."

There was a flicker of unease in Diego's eyes, and he glanced around the farm quickly before looking back at her. "You're lying."

"Am I?' Cocking an eyebrow, Rayna went on, "Not only that, but the man you sent to the Caldwell's up the road is also sitting in jail. They are all turning over evidence on you as we speak."

"Looks like you are the only one left." Ryder's voice rang out from behind her, "The two in the barn didn't quite make it out, and it doesn't look like the ones out here fared any better."

Taking advantage of the distraction, Rayna kicked out, connecting with the gun in Diego's hand, and sending it flying. He rushed forward, grabbing her and yanking her into his arms, her back against his chest. She felt the bite of a knife in her side, as she locked eyes with Ryder. He held his gun leveled on them, not lowering it, even with the threat to her life. He trusted her. He knew she would want to go down fighting, no matter what, she could see it in his eyes.

"Hiding behind a woman, Diego?" Ryder said, shaking his head. "Rayna was right, you really are nothing but a coward."

Rayna smiled at the sound of sirens coming their way. Here comes the cavalry. Too bad it would be over before they got there.

"I've had enough of you bitch! Say hi to your parents for me!" Rayna felt the knife cut into her, but she didn't let the sharp pain stop her. Slamming her elbow into his side, she threw her head back connecting with his face. There was a satisfying crunch, and then she twisted around, grabbing his arms and wrestling him to the ground. Diego lost the knife in their struggle, and soon Rayna had him on his stomach, and she was straddling him. "You bastard," she yelled, digging her knee into the center of his back. "I should fucking kill you for what you did to me."

"Do it!" he sneered. "You don't have the balls!"

"That's where you are wrong," she said, slamming his head into the ground. "I just choose not to kill unless it's absolutely necessary. Besides, the thought of you rotting away in prison seems like a better idea to me."

"I agree." Ryder said, jumping over the side of the gazebo to get to her quickly. "Besides, where he's going, he probably won't last a month."

Hearing a soft moan behind her, Rayna turned to look at the boy who had just saved her life. She wanted to go to him, but she refused to let up at all on Diego until he was in a pair of cuffs.

Nickolas was silent when the authorities arrived to take away his father. Rayna stayed by his side until the EMTs showed up to take him to the hospital. Wishing that she could go with him, but knowing she needed to stay behind for questioning and to file her report, she promised Nickolas that she would be there soon. She saw the disbelief in his gaze before he turned away, blocking her out.

Chapter 39

Rayna's boots clicked loudly on the hospital floor as she made her way down the hall toward Nickolas's room. She was exhausted. After three hours with the FBI and Serenity Springs police department, she and Ryder spent another hour at his place with his parents. The man his mother shot was going to live, and Cara seemed to be doing fine, but they were worried about Ryder's father. Even though the doctors had looked Charles over, they wanted someone to keep an eye on him throughout the night, just to make sure the stress wasn't too much on his heart.

With the fear of another heart attack on their minds, none of his family wanted to leave his side. Creed and Katy had decided to split the time, so he was at the ranch now, while she was on duty. Caiden was also at the house, and Rayna had left Ryder with them, promising to call him as soon as she made it home, no matter what time it was. She didn't want to leave him, but she could not just abandon Nickolas at the hospital. She knew what it was like to be in pain, in a room by yourself, with no family, and no one who really cared about you. She would not leave Nickolas alone like that.

There were two deputies posted outside Nickolas's door, and she could see Katy talking to a doctor in the small waiting room not far away. "Is that really necessary?" she asked by way of greeting. "I'm sure the kid isn't going to get up and run away after all that he's been through."

"It's for his protection," Katy said, before smiling and thanking the doctor. Turning back to Rayna after he left, she continued, "I just want to make sure that his dickhead dad doesn't have any more of his goons around that could harm him."

Rayna rubbed a hand over her eyes wearily. "Thanks. I'm sorry, Katy. I just know what Nickolas is going through. I should have been here before now. He probably thinks I've forgotten about him."

Katy slipped an arm around Rayna's shoulder, pulling her in for a quick hug, before backing away. "Then I'm glad he has you in his corner. He's going to need someone."

Rayna glanced over when she heard footsteps coming down the hall, relieved when she saw Nathan and Harper. "Thank God," she breathed. Knowing they were alright, and actually seeing it with her own eyes, were two different things.

Nathan stopped beside her, nodding stiffly to both her and Katy. Rayna cringed inwardly at the tension rolling off both him and Harper. They stood a distance apart from one another, keeping their eyes on Rayna. "We are certain all of Cortez's men have been apprehended," Nathan said, his voice full of authority, definitely the FBI agent now, and not Nate Burrows. "Nickolas should be safe now."

"And Lyssa?" Rayna questioned.

Nathan's eyes turned glacier hard, and one of his hands clenched tightly into a fist. "She's been life-flighted to a hospital in Dallas. She's in critical condition. They don't know if she is going to make it."

Rayna held back tears as she sat down in one of the chairs near her. "It's my fault," she whispered. "If I hadn't come here, if I hadn't pushed to bring Diego down, Lyssa wouldn't be in this situation. Nickolas wouldn't be hurting."

"Stop right there," Nathan said gruffly, walking over to sit beside her. "Diego Cortez is a piece of shit, Rayna. He preys on others for his own enjoyment. Not only did you manage to capture him, but you took down a lot of his crew too. Think of all the lives you saved that they would have taken in the future. I am sure Lyssa would agree that whatever happens, taking him out of the picture was worth it." When Rayna would have protested, Nathan reached over and took her hand in his. "As for that boy in there, you saved his life too."

"No," she whispered, "he saved mine. He jumped in front of me to take a bullet that was meant for me, Nathan."

"Yes, and he is a fucking hero for it. Don't take that away from him, Rayna. You go in there and you tell him how proud you are of him, just like I'm telling you right now. I am so damn proud of you, Rayna Williams. You are one of the best agents I have ever worked with, and I would want you on my side any time."

Rayna swallowed hard, covering his hand with hers. "Thank you, Nathan. You don't know what that means to me." Looking at Harper, she said, "I heard Barker and Masters ended up on your ranch after their visit to Lyssa. I'm so sorry, Harper."

Harper's gaze went from her to Nathan, then back again. "Don't be, Rayna. Nate filled me in on what's been going on. I'm just glad they caught the bastards so you can live your life in freedom now."

"Thank God none of the children were there when they showed up," Katy said, "although it looked like you were doing just fine when I got there."

A short burst of laughter left Nathan, as he looked at Harper for the first time since they arrived, pride in his eyes. "She had them hogtied and waiting for me by the time I got there. Remind me not to mess with her in the future."

Rayna saw Harper flinch before she replied, "I was just protecting what's mine."

Something was definitely not right between Nate and Harper, but it wasn't her place to interfere. Standing, Rayna smiled, "I think it's time we went to check on Nickolas. He needs to know he isn't alone in all of this."

"I agree," Harper said. "I would like to go with you, if you don't mind."

"Of course not. I think your expertise will help in this situation."

They made their way down the hall to Nickolas's room, Katy and Nathan following close behind. The deputies nodded at them as they entered the room, not moving from their posts. Nickolas lay in the bed staring out the window beside him. He sported a stark white bandage where the bullet had entered his shoulder. From what the doctor said, he was lucky because it was a clean shot that went straight through, hitting nothing vital. After some physical therapy, he would be just fine.

"Hey there," Rayna said, walking over to Nickolas, "Sorry it took so long for me to get here. I had to take care of some things first."

"Like putting my father in jail."

It wasn't a question, and she decided honesty was the best policy. "Yes, Nickolas. It's where he belongs."

He finally turned to look at her, and her heart filled with compassion at the lost look in his eyes. "And me? Is that where I belong too?"

"No," she said softly, sitting down beside him and taking his hand in hers.

"How do you know? Maybe I'm just like him."

Squeezing his hand, Rayna smiled. "I know a lot about you, Nickolas Matthew Cortez. I know that you love to read. You read everything you can get your hands on, both fiction and non-fiction. I know that you sketch beautiful pictures. I know that you excel in school, getting straight A's." Reaching out, she cradled his chin in her hand, "And I know you are a good person. A very good person. You are nothing like your father, Nickolas. You are your own person, and now you get to build your own life, just the way you want it."

Nickolas's jaw clenched, and he admitted, "I've hurt people before. I didn't want to, but he made me."

"I know that too," Rayna said, letting go of his jaw to ruffle his hair. "I also know that it was against your will."

"I should have done something."

"You did," Nathan interjected from where he stood leaning against the far wall. "You saved Rayna's life today, Nickolas. You stood up to your father, and took a bullet meant for her. That means something."

Nickolas looked over at Nathan, and she could see the war he was fighting inside. "That doesn't make up for what I've done in the past."

"No," Nathan agreed, "but you have the rest of your life for that. It's your choice how you live it, but you took a step in the right direction today, kid. I have confidence that you will prove to be the man I know you can be."

Nickolas's gaze went from him, to Harper, to Rayna, before he nodded. "I'm not my father."

"No," Rayna said, patting his hand gently, "you are not."

Nickolas was quiet for a moment before he said, "If I'm not going to prison, does that mean I will be put in foster care?"

"That's where I come in," Harper responded, stepping forward.

"Are you a social worker?"

"No, I'm not." Harper smiled, placing her hands on her hips and lifting an eyebrow. "Do I look like a social worker?"

A small smile lifted the corner of Nickolas's mouth. "No, not really. Not like any of the ones I've seen on TV anyway."

Harper laughed, shaking her head. "You got that right, Nicky my boy, I am definitely not like the ones you see on TV."

"Harper," Nathan interrupted, "can I talk to you outside for a minute?"

"No." Her response was quick and decisive, before she looked back at Nickolas. "I own a place called New Hope Ranch just a few miles outside of town. I have several kids like you that live on that ranch with me, Nickolas. Kids that have nowhere else to go."

"Kids that no one else wants, you mean."

"Not exactly." Harper smiled gently now, going to stand beside the bed. "Some of them have families who love them very much, but they are going through things that their family is unable to help them through. Some of them come from abusive homes, some have no one. I don't discriminate on my ranch. If you need help, for any reason, I'm there."

Nickolas looked at her in confusion. "I don't understand."

"Nickolas, I'm offering you a place to live. A place where you will have to help out with chores, where you will have to go to school daily, a place where you will be challenged to be the best person that you can be. But, also a place where you will fit in and know that someone is always there for you, no matter what."

"You?" he whispered.

"Yes."

"And me too," Rayna promised, squeezing his hand again. "I live just a few miles away."

"You aren't leaving?" Nickolas asked, turning his hand over to clutch at hers.

"I will have to for a little while, but when I come back, it will be for good," Rayna promised.

"You will never have to be alone, Nickolas. We will be here for you." She would make sure of it.

"I don't know if a judge will sign off on this," Nathan said, straightening away from the wall.

"He will," Harper said, glaring at him, "because you are going to make sure it happens."

Nathan looked from Harper's demanding gaze, to Rayna's pleading one, before muttering, "Women." Shaking her head, Harper left the room, Nathan quickly following.

"I'm glad to hear you're staying, Rayna," Katy said. "There's a job waiting for you at the station if you are interested. I talked to Creed about it already. I'm planning on leaving town soon, and I'm not sure how long I will be gone. We could really use you."

"Ryder told me that you plan on looking for your birth parents. Do you know when you will be going?"

"As soon as I know Creed will be okay without me. I don't want to leave him in a bind." Her eyes sparkling with humor, Katy said, "That's where you come in."

Rayna laughed, "I will definitely think about it. Thank you, Katy, and I wish you luck. If you need help with anything, let me know. I may have some resources that you don't."

Katy nodded, and for the first time Rayna saw hesitancy in her eyes. "I just hope I'm doing the right thing."

"Does it feel right?"

"Yes." Katy looked out the window, crossing her arms over her chest. "I have always wanted to look into my past. But now…I don't know…it's different. Now I feel like I *have* to. Something is pushing at me, telling me I can't wait any longer."

"Then don't fight it," Rayna told her. "Go. We will all be here for you when you get back."

Katy whispered, "Thank you, Rayna. I think I just needed someone to talk to." Walking to the door, she glanced back with a smile, "I better get back to work. Thanks again."

"Anytime."

Watching Katy go, Rayna realized Nickolas's hand had slackened in hers, and she looked down to see that he had fallen asleep. Smiling, she whispered, "You are going to be just fine, Nickolas. I promise."

"Harper! Dammit, Harper, wait up!" Nathan skirted around a car, barely jumping out of the way in time to miss another one coming his way, before finally catching up to her, where she was getting ready to slide into her Ford truck. Catching her hand in his, he rasped, "Talk to me."

Harper stopped, one hand on the wheel, and turned back to look at him. "The counselors will be back with the children soon, Nate."

"Nathan," he interjected.

"What?"

"My name is Nathan. Nathan Brentworth."

Harper shook her head, looking away. After several moments she whispered, "I don't even know you."

"Give me a chance to change that," he all but begged, and Nathan did *not* beg. "Let me show you the real me."

His grip on her hand tightened while he waited for her reply, his heart sinking when she finally turned back to him, her response there in her eyes. "I'm sorry, Nathan. You put my children in danger. Even if I could look past the lies, I just can't forgive you for that." Tugging her hand from his, Harper jumped into the truck, slamming the door shut behind her. Rolling the window down, she started the vehicle, putting it into gear. With one last look, she whispered, "Goodbye."

Chapter 40

Two days later, Ryder knocked on Rayna's door, his heart in his throat, praying what Katy had told him the day before was true. Was Rayna really staying in Serenity Springs? Was she giving up everything she knew in Virginia? Leaving the FBI? God, he hoped so. He could not imagine his life without her in it.

The door opened, and Rayna stood on the other side. "Wow," he whispered. She was stunning, with her hair loose around her shoulders, a dress that accented her curves to perfection, and a pair of dark brown cowboy boots, boots he vowed would stay on later, but nothing else. "You are so beautiful."

Rayna's cheeks flushed a pretty pink, just the way he loved them to, and she ducked her head shyly. "Thank you." Opening the door wider, she said, "I have dinner ready if you would like some?"

"You cooked?" he asked in surprise.

"Not exactly," Rayna admitted with a laugh. "But I did everything else."

He glanced past her, beyond the living room to the dining room, which now had a nice sized table in it. There were two tall candles on each end, lit and shining brightly. Removing his Stetson, he hung it up on a hook by the door before walking to the dining room. There were two place settings, both filled with steak, potatoes, corn, and what looked like homemade bread. "Everything looks wonderful, Rayna." It was perfect.

"Good," Rayna replied, a delighted grin on her face. The woman was full of contradictions. One moment a tough FBI agent ready to take down the biggest, meanest, mob boss in town, the next sweet and shy, worried about pleasing others. Then there was the sexy, sensual side of her, the one she saved only for him. He could not wait to see that side of her tonight. After what they'd been through, and then not seeing her for two days, he needed to feel her close.

"Let's eat before it gets cold," she said, motioning toward the table.

Pulling out a chair, Ryder waited until Rayna sat, before leaning down to kiss her gently on the neck, right below her ear. "Do you know how amazing you are?"

He was close enough to feel the shudder ripple through her as she responded, "I'm not amazing. I'm just me."

"You are everything," he said, kissing her gently on the lips before taking his own seat.

Dinner was good, the company was better, and soon they were clearing the table and doing the dishes together. He wanted this every night with her. Dinner, dishes, laughter, love. He wanted it all.

"Ryder."

He paused at the serious tone in her voice, placing the dishtowel he was drying his hands off with beside the sink. "Yes?"

"I'm leaving for Virginia tomorrow morning."

His heart stopped and he felt as if his entire world were falling down around him. "You're leaving?"

"Yes. Nathan said he was heading out tonight, but I wanted to see you before I go."

"I thought…" he couldn't get the words out. She was leaving him?

"What?'

Turning from her, he stalked out of the kitchen into the dining room. He was aware of her following him, but he didn't stop until she grabbed his arm.

"Ryder, what's wrong?"

Looking down at her hand, he ground out, "Katy said you were staying."

Rayna stepped in front of him, cradling his face in her hands, "Oh, Ryder. I should have handled this better." His eyes met hers, and hope slowly began to build at what he saw. "I have to leave for now, but I'm coming back. I am going to Virginia to hand in my resignation to my boss. I need to pack up my apartment and pay off my lease. And I need to visit my family's gravesite to say goodbye." She smiled tremulously, "This is my home, Ryder. I'm going to submit my application to Creed for one of the deputy positions he has open, and I'm going to live here."

Unable to hear anymore, Ryder lowered his head and covered her mouth with his. She was staying, that was all he needed to know. Sliding his hands under her dress, he cupped her ass, picking her up and turning to place her on the table. She moaned as he lightly stroked a hand up her thigh, pushing her dress up higher and higher. He had to touch her. Had to feel her soft, silky skin against his. *She was coming back to him.*

Rayna undid the button of his jeans, and Ryder groaned in pleasure when she slipped her fingers inside to find his cock. Taking his hands from her just long enough to slide the jeans down his hips, he groaned, "I need to be inside you, Rayna."

"Yes," she gasped, throwing her head back in pleasure when he slipped the strap of her dress down, baring her breast to his hungry gaze. Cupping it in his palm, he captured the nipple in his mouth, sucking gently. Her cries pushed him closer to the edge, and he quickly reached down to remove her panties, reveling in the feel of her fingers moving on his throbbing cock.

Letting go of her breast, Ryder grasped her hips and pulled her closer, positioning himself at her hot core, before slowly pushing his way inside. She felt so good…so right…so perfect. "Rayna," he rasped, as he began moving slowly in and out of her, "you are everything to me."

He saw her eyes widen in wonder, then her head fell back as she clutched his shoulders, wrapping her legs around his hips and pulling him deeper into her. "Ryder!"

He tried to make it last, knowing this one night would have to last several days, if not weeks. But the soft pants coming from her lips, her cries of pleasure, the bite of her nails in his shoulders, were all too much, and soon he gave into the need to come, with Rayna quickly following.

They stayed locked together for several minutes afterwards, foreheads resting against each other, trying to catch their breath. Finally, Ryder stepped back, pulling his jeans up. Before she could move, he gathered her into his arms and carried her upstairs. In her bedroom, he removed her clothes and his, then slid under the covers with her. The rest of the night was spent making love and holding each other tight, morning coming way too soon.

Ryder woke to the sun shining through the curtains, the bed empty except for him. There was a note on Rayna's pillow, and he sighed in disappointment as he opened it. He would have liked to hold her one last time, kissed her, told her how much he loved her. Which made him realize that he never had actually said those three little words to her. Holding the note in front of him, he read:

Ryder,

I loved the sweet boy who took time out of his day to write me a song and make me feel special years ago, and I love the man who stands beside me in life and death now. Until I see you again,

Rayna

Chapter 41

"I don't want to accept this," Assistant Director Talbot groused, looking at the resignation Rayna just set on his desk. "You are one of my best agents."

Rayna smiled, placing her badge next to the letter. "It's what is best for me, Sir. My life is in Serenity Springs now."

Talbot pushed his chair away from the desk, standing. "I was afraid that was going to happen, but I'm happy for you Rayna. Or is it Macey now that Cortez is behind bars?"

She had wondered that same thing, but it didn't take long for her to figure out her answer. "Rayna," she said with a smile. "A part of me will always be Macey Fuller, the young girl who loved to read and write, and live in a fantasy world. But I'm Rayna Williams now. I'm stronger, wiser, and happier. I make my own fairytales come true."

The assistant director laughed, coming around the desk to give her a brief hug. "You are definitely one of the strongest people I know. I wish you all of the happiness in the world, Rayna. If you ever need anything, anything at all, you call me."

Rayna left Talbot's office with a spring in her step and a smile on her face. It was finally over. All of it. They'd found the mole in the office. One of the secretaries who had worked for the agency for over ten years. Diego had threatened her family, and she'd done what she thought she needed to do to keep them safe. Now, unfortunately, she was facing charges and could get put away for the rest of her life. She promised them she would cooperate and tell them everything she could. Her family was safe now, and that was all that mattered to her.

Lyssa Taylor was going to make it, but it was going to be a long, hard struggle for her. Scars now marred her skin, and fear had settled deep in her heart, causing horrible nightmares. It would take a lot of counseling and hard work on her part, but Rayna knew Lyssa would pull through. Rayna had left her number with the woman after visiting her in the hospital, offering her a room in her home at Serenity Springs, if she ever needed to get away. Since the small town was where the attack took place, Rayna wasn't sure if she would accept the offer, but it was there in case she needed it.

On her way out of the FBI building, Rayna ran into Special Agent Nathan Brentworth. She hadn't seen him in the two weeks she'd been back, and assumed he was on another assignment. "Hey Nathan," she greeted him. "How have you been?"

"Getting ready to go undercover again," was his response. "I have no idea how long this one will take."

"I wish you luck, my friend."

"Thanks." Nathan stood there for a moment before he said, "Do me a favor, Rayna?"

"Anything."

"Keep an eye on Harper for me." She saw the sadness that entered his eyes before he quickly masked it.

"She still won't talk to you?" Rayna guessed, wishing that Harper would give him a chance. She understood that Harper was looking out for the children on her ranch, but Nathan was a good man, and Rayna hated to see him look so beat down.

"No, she won't accept my calls," he admitted.

Rayna placed a hand on his arm, "I promise I will watch out for both her and Nickolas." When Nathan turned to go, she said, "Thank you for what you did for Nickolas, Nathan. I know he would not be at New Hope Ranch if it wasn't for you."

Nathan shrugged, "He's a good kid. He deserves a chance at a different life than the one he was originally dealt."

"Thank you," she said again, then watched him walk away, his head down as if he had the weight of the world on his shoulders.

Wishing there was something she could do for the man who had risked everything and lost so much, Rayna sighed, deciding the only thing she could do was watch out for the woman he cared about.

Leaving the FBI for the last time, Rayna drove to the cemetery to say goodbye to her family. She was planning on leaving the next day for Serenity Springs, and wanted to get an early start. This was the last thing on her list of things to do today, and she'd waited as long as she could to stop by, knowing it would be the hardest.

Pulling through the gates, she slowly made her way around the outside of all of the gravesites, parking near her family plot. Getting out of the car, she took the roses from the passenger seat, and made her way to their graves. She was almost there, when she stopped in confusion at the sight of the woman standing in front of her parents' tombstone, a small boy holding her hand. All Rayna could see was her long blonde hair, and tall, slender build from behind. Then the boy turned to look at her, and Rayna gasped, dropping the roses to the ground as she covered her mouth with her hands. He was the spitting image of her little brother. Blonde hair, green eyes, freckles across his nose. "Matty."

The little boy cocked his head to the side, a small smile forming, "How do you know my name?"

As Rayna stood there in shock, the woman turned to look at her. Dark green eyes to match her son's, features mirroring Rayna's mother's, similar to her own. "Macey?"

"Olivia." It was her sister! She was alive! Rayna's eyes misted over as she looked from Olivia to the little boy. Olivia's son.

Olivia walked over to her, holding out her arms. "Come here, baby sis. I have missed you so much."

Rayna let out a sob, allowing Olivia to enfold her into her arms. Her sister was *alive*! Did that mean the rest of her family was as well? Pulling back, she looked around, "Daddy? Momma? Matty?"

"No, it's just me," Olivia said quietly. "They are all gone."

"I'm here, Mommy," the little boy said. "I'm not gone."

Olivia laughed softly, "Yes, this is true, Matty. You are definitely here."

"I don't understand," Rayna whispered. Unable to stop herself, she pulled Matty close for a hug, surprised when he didn't resist.

"You and I are the only ones who survived so many years ago," Olivia explained, placing her hand on Rayna's shoulder. "After talking to the U.S. Marshals, I agreed to allow them to split us up. I didn't want to leave you, Macey, but it was the safest thing for both of us."

Rayna glared up at her, "It wasn't your decision to make Olivia. I needed you."

"Actually, yes it was. I was eighteen, you were seventeen. Technically, I was your guardian."

Her hand tightening on Rayna's shoulder, she said, "You can be as mad at me as you want, little sister, but I don't regret my decision. I love you, and would do anything for you, even leave you if it meant you would be safe."

Rayna rose, looking down when Matty slipped his hand in hers. "We are a family now, Aunt Macey," he grinned.

"Aunt Rayna," she corrected gently. "My name is Rayna now."

"Mommy's is Charity," Matty told her. "Isn't that pretty?"

"Yes," Rayna agreed, looking at her sister with a smile. "It's very pretty."

Olivia held out a hand to her, and Rayna took it without hesitation. "We just flew in from San Diego. I couldn't wait to see you, and to finally be able to pay my respects to Dad, Mom, and our little brother."

"You live in California?" Rayna remembered that Olivia always wanted to move to California or New York when she was younger. "And are you a photographer too?" She prayed her sister's dreams had come true, and that she had happiness and love in her life over the past twelve years.

"She takes lots and lots of pictures all of the time," Matty told her, his eyes opened wide.

Olivia laughed, "Yes, I do, but that is a story for another time. Matty and I need to find a place to stay while we are in town. I was thinking the Hilton on Greensboro Avenue?"

"Why don't you both stay with me?" Rayna offered. "I have a lot to tell you."

Chapter 42

Ryder spoke quietly to Cochise as he ran the brush over his back, but his thoughts were on the woman who left six weeks ago and still hadn't returned. He missed her so fucking much. He should have told her how much he loved her before letting her go. Hell, he should never have let her go in the first place. He was a fool.

"I'm an idiot, Cochise," he muttered, resting his hand against the horse's back. "She's the best thing that's ever happened to me, and I let her just leave. What was I thinking?" Cochise neighed softly, turning his head to look back at him. Ryder chuckled, "Yeah, buddy. I'm a dumbass, I know. I never should have let her go." Running his hand down the animal's neck, he told him, "I'm giving her one more week, then I'm going to go find her and bring her home where she belongs."

"Why wait a week?"

The gentle voice was filled with amusement, and something else. All Ryder knew was that it wasn't the voice he wanted to hear. "Because when you love someone, you give them their space," he responded, placing the brush down on the railing beside where he stood and turning toward the open barn doors. A petite, curvy woman stood there, her long blonde hair curling over her shoulders and around her waist, laughter in her deep green eyes.

"And what if they find someone else when you are giving them all of that space?" she teased.

Ryder walked slowly toward her, a grin appearing on his lips, "She won't."

"How can you be sure?"

"Because she loves me," he said simply, "and when Rayna loves someone, she does it with all of her heart." Stopping, he held his arms open, pulling her close when she stepped into them.

"Hello, Ryder," she breathed against his chest, snuggling close.

"It's good to see you again, Olivia."

Olivia leaned back, smiling up at him. "That's a name I haven't heard in a long time. I go by Charity now."

Stepping back, Ryder held her hands as he looked down at her. "You look great, Charity," he replied. "and the name fits you."

Olivia giggled, "It will take some getting used to for you and your family, I'm sure, but even though Diego is gone now, I'm going to keep it. Olivia is who I used to be, Charity is who I have become."

Ryder nodded in understanding. "Tell me a little about who you are now."

Olivia…no, Charity…he was going to have to get used to it, let go of his hands and walked over to sit on a bale of hay in the corner of the barn. “Well, where should I start?”

Wondering where Rayna was, Ryder followed Charity and sat down beside her. “From the beginning is always best.”

Charity cocked her head to the side, staring at him, “You don’t seem surprised to see me alive, Ryder.”

“When you have gone through everything I’ve gone through these past few months with your sister, nothing tends to surprise you,” he said, leaning forward and resting his elbows on his legs. Shaking his head, he shrugged, “If she survived the accident, it stands to reason some of the rest of your family may have as well.” He looked at the door, wishing Rayna would walk through it. He wanted to see her, to hold her close. And once he got her near again, he wasn’t letting her go.

“You know, you could go see my sister, Ryder. She’s just outside with your family. We can talk later.”

The desire to stand up and go to the woman he loved was almost too strong to deny. “No,” he finally said, shaking his head, “Tell me about you.”

Charity’s eyes were filled with laughter, a wide smile on her face, “Let me make this fast for you, Ryder. After the accident, the U.S. Marshals moved me to San Diego, California to live. I got married at twenty-two to a man whom I loved very much. He passed away three years ago, but we have a son together. Matty is six now."

"You named him after your brother."

"Yes," Charity whispered, her eyes clouding over. "And before you ask, Macey and I are the only ones who survived."

"Rayna," he interjected.

"What?"

"She goes by Rayna now. It's what she prefers."

"That's right," Charity agreed. "Sometimes it's hard to remember, because even though you know her now as Rayna, my heart knows her as Macey."

"Mine knows her as both," Ryder said, rising. "And it can't wait any longer to find her. I'm sorry."

"Go," Charity replied, pointing toward the door. "Go make my sister happy. She's been silent for the past hour. I'm sure she's worried about how you feel about her."

Ryder didn't need to be told twice. Walking out of the barn, he looked around, his gaze quickly skimming over his family, and a small, towhead boy playing with his niece, Cassie. His eyes finally settled on the person he was looking for, standing with her arms on the corral fence, looking out over the pasture land beyond. A feeling of completeness settled over him as he forced himself to walk, not run, to her.

Rayna waited quietly by the fence for Ryder and her sister to make an appearance. It had only been fifteen minutes, maybe twenty, since Olivia went into the barn, but it felt like a lifetime. All of Rayna's insecurities returned where Ryder and Olivia were concerned. Olivia was the one he loved years ago. Would he decide she was the one for him now? And what would Rayna do if he did? She'd given up her position with the FBI to come live in Serenity Springs with him. Even though he never told her he loved her, she was praying he did and wanted to spend his life with her. Now what would happen?

Rayna jumped when she felt strong arms go around her waist, pulling her back against a firm, hard chest. She shivered when she felt Ryder's breath on her neck, right before he placed a soft kiss behind her ear. "You're home."

Settling back against him, she smiled. He still wanted her, and it felt so right to be in his arms again. "Did you miss me?"

Ryder nuzzled the skin of her neck, placing kisses down to her shoulder, "More than you know."

"My sister's alive," she whispered. "No one else survived, but she did."

"I see that," the gentle kisses never stopped. "I'm happy for you, sweetheart."

"Ryder…"

Ryder turned her around in his arms, sliding his fingers through her hair. "Rayna, I know what you are thinking, but there is nothing in this world that is going to keep me from you."

Rayna's eyes filled with tears, "Nothing?"

"Nothing," Ryder promised, covering her lips with his. She moaned softly, a shudder going through her body. She had been so afraid she was going to lose him. Pulling back, Ryder raised his head, his blue eyes full of promise, "Your sister may have held a piece of my heart in the past, Rayna Williams, but you own me now, heart and soul. There is nothing in this world I wouldn't do for you."

Rayna's eyes widened when Ryder knelt before her, removing something from his jeans pocket. "I've been carrying around this thing since before you left," he admitted, opening a dark blue velvet box. A lone solitaire diamond sat inside, the sun glinting off of it, making it sparkle and shine. Grasping one of her hands in his, he kissed the back of it, smiling up at her again. "Will you put me out of my misery, Rayna Williams, and make me the happiest man alive?"

Rayna didn't bother to fight the tears that flowed freely down her cheeks. She had been through hell most of her life, running from a man who wanted to destroy her entire family. But, now that man was gone, and she only had one more place to run.

Straight into Ryder's arms. "Yes!" she managed to gasp through her tears. "Yes, Ryder, yes!"

Ryder removed the ring from the box, placing it on her finger. Then he let out a loud whoop as he stood, picking her up in his arms and twirling her around in a circle. Rayna heard laughter and cheers coming from behind them, but when Ryder's lips connected with hers, everything went away except for him. Yes, she was finally home.

Acknowledgements

In Saving His Soul, I mention two of my favorite authors, and very good friends, Tiffany J. West and Heather Dahlgren. We have been friends for over a year now, and I do not know what I would do without them. Thank you, Tiffany, for letting me reference your Downtown series in my book, and thank you Heather for allowing me to mention your Sexy Series. Both series are copyrighted by said authors.

Thank you to my models, William Scott and T. H. Snyder, and to my photographer, Shauna Kruse, for making my vision come to life with your amazing photo shoot.

My cover designer, Kari Ayasha, once again came up with the perfect cover. Thank you so much! You always seem to know just what I am envisioning, or hoping for.

A huge thank you to all of my Beta readers. You are all absolutely wonderful, and I really appreciate everything you do for me. (Jessica, Charmarie, Tabitha, Karrie, Kathy, Staci, Jamie, Marie)

About the Author

I have a wonderful, supportive husband and three beautiful children. I enjoy spending time with all of them which normally involves some baseball, shooting hoops, taking walks, watching movies, and of course reading.

My passion for reading began at a very young age and only grew over time. Whether I was bringing home a book from the library, or sneaking one of my mom's romance novels and reading by the light in the hallway when we were supposed to be sleeping, I always had a book.

I read several different genres and subgenres, but Paranormal Romance and Romantic Suspense have always been my favorites.

I have always made up my own stories, and have just recently decided to start sharing them. I hope everyone enjoys reading them as much as I enjoy writing them.

~~ Dawn

82807164R00165

Made in the USA
Lexington, KY
06 March 2018